W9-BBN-910

# MAKOONS

# ALSO BY LOUISE ERDRICH

## FOR CHILDREN

Grandmother's Pigeon
ILLUSTRATED BY JIM LAMARCHE

The Range Eternal
ILLUSTRATED BY STEVE JOHNSON AND LOU FANCHER

The Birchbark House

The Game of Silence

The Porcupine Year

Chickadee

## NOVELS AND STORIES

Love Medicine

The Beet Queen

Tracks

The Bingo Palace

Tales of Burning Love

The Antelope Wife

The Last Report on the Miracles at Little No Horse

The Master Butchers Singing Club

Four Souls

The Painted Drum

The Plague of Doves

The Red Convertible

Shadow Tag

The Round House

## POETRY

Jacklight

Baptism of Desire

Original Fire

## NONFICTION

The Blue Jay's Dance

Books and Islands in Ojibwe Country

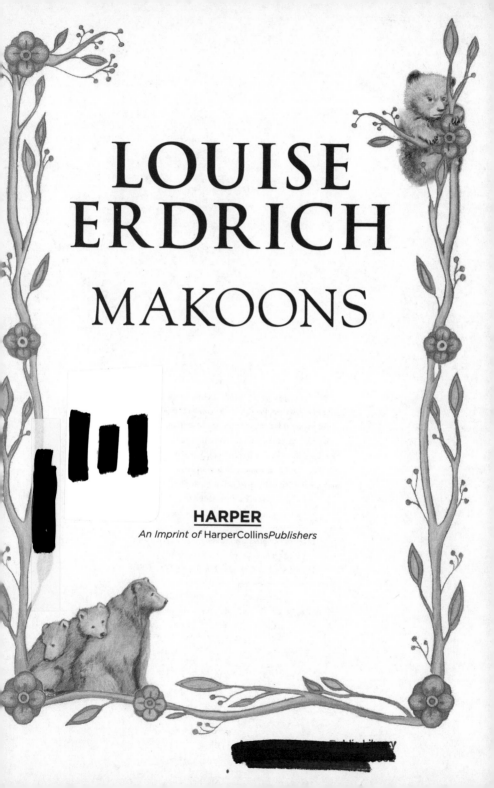

# LOUISE ERDRICH

## MAKOONS

**HARPER**
*An Imprint of HarperCollinsPublishers*

Makoons

Copyright © 2016 by Louise Erdrich

All rights reserved. Printed in the United States of America.
No part of this book may be used or reproduced in any
manner whatsoever without written permission except in
the case of brief quotations embodied in critical articles and
reviews. For information address HarperCollins Children's
Books, a division of HarperCollins Publishers, 195 Broadway,
New York, NY 10007.
www.harpercollinschildrens.com

Library of Congress Control Number: 2015038741
ISBN 978-0-06-057793-3 (trade bdg.)
ISBN 978-0-06-057794-0 (lib bdg.)

Typography by Andrea Vandergrift
16 17 18 19 20  PC/RRDH  10 9 8 7 6 5 4 3 2 1

First Edition

*To Eliza Jonis Burke Erdrich*

# CONTENTS

DAKOTA
TERRITORY

Turtle Mountains

(This beautiful land of richly
wooded hills became the
home reservation of the
ancestors'
family
and the pretty mother
of the author)

The valiant and surprising
journey of a changed
man and a little girl

A tiny representation of the vast
herds of mashkode-bizhikiwag
or buffalo who roamed the
Great Plains

PEMBINA c. 1866

MAKOONS

Makoons means bear cub.
This boy is a dreamer and
a bold, fearless rider.

Wolves wait for a chance

RED RIVER of the North

# THE VISION

Makoons opened his weak eyes, blinked, and saw himself as he used to be—a boy glowing with strength and health. He closed his eyes and heard a voice singing the way he used to sing—a voice full and pure. The hand on his arm felt like his old hand, before the sickness—capable, excited, concerned. Makoons opened his eyes again, and saw his twin brother. He struggled to rise but weakness fixed him in his blankets. The voice continued. *Small things have great power*, his brother sang to him. The notes were sweetly cheerful. Makoons closed his eyes and took a deep breath. He smiled. Chickadee, his twin, the other half of his soul, had returned, and Makoons was going to get well.

The boys were born in the thaw of late winter, when steam ravels from the dens of bears to signal their birth. Makwa is the Ojibwe word for "bear." Makoons is the word for "little bear," or bear cub. Makoons had grown ill when his twin was kidnapped and taken away. He recovered once his twin returned. The boys were connected to each other by invisible strings of life. They understood each other like nobody else, and also they annoyed each other like nobody else. Makoons knew that his brother slept beside him now, fed him from a spoon made from a buffalo horn. His brother continued to sing to him until his voice changed from the trill of the chickadee to the harsh and ragged croak of the crow. Still, Chickadee kept on, healing his brother song by song.

One morning when the two boys were alone, Makoons stared from the blankets at Chickadee and whispered.

"Brother, I have seen something."

"What did you see?"

"Last night, I was hot with fever. I could not eat. I was staring out at nothing, when my mind was strangely opened. I saw all that is to happen. I still see it, brother."

"Tell me," said Chickadee.

"I am going to get well," said Makoons, "but that is not important. We will become strong and bring down buffalo. We'll have horses; we'll feed our people. All of us will travel into the great grass places, toward the western stars. We will never go back east to our lake, our deep woods."

Chickadee's heart pinched, for he loved the trees and water of his old home.

"My brother," said Makoons. "That isn't all. We will be tested, too."

"What is going to happen?" Chickadee sat very still in the blankets, a spoon poised in one hand. A bowl of buffalo broth was cupped in the other hand.

"I can't see exactly," said Makoons. "But I know we will have to save them."

"Save who?"

"Our family. Only . . ."

"Only what?"

"Only," said Makoons. His voice failed, tears squeezed from the corners of his eyes. His voice dropped so low that Chickadee had to bend close to hear it.

"My brother," Makoons whispered. "We cannot save them all."

So it began—the living out of this vision—which Makoons saw in the early summer of 1866.

# ONE

## WHIRLWIND AND SWEETHEART

M akoons, the Bear Child, had a way with horses. Since his family had moved from the deep woods, across the Red River and onto the Great Plains, horses had replaced canoes. There weren't enough rivers on the grassland. The beautiful birchbark canoes made with such care by Makoons's parents and grandparents were now abandoned, sliding back into the earth, or paddled by strangers in the lakes and rivers of what was now the state of Minnesota. Out here, Dakota Territory still belonged to the buffalo, the hunters of the buffalo, to the wolves and the eagles. Back in Minnesota the Ojibwe, or Anishinaabeg, were being forced to settle on small pieces of their old hunting grounds. Yellow Kettle, and the other old people, called those pieces of land the ishoniganan, or leftovers. The U.S. government, the settlers, and the farmers in Minnesota called them reservations. The Plains were immense, treeless, with different laws, but they were not yet parceled out into the hands of settlers. The Ojibwe, the Cree, the Dakota, Nakota, Lakota, and other indigenous peoples did not yet have to live on the leftovers.

The spotted pony that Makoons had tamed grew big and strong. He called his horse Whirlwind because the hair on its forehead, a white blaze on red-brown hide, made a whirling pattern, as did the cloudy patch along his flank. Now the twins' father, Animikiins, watched as Makoons rode hard at a great buffalo hide hanging off a pliant sapling. The two of them had concocted this idea in order to train the pony. He would be a buffalo pony. Fearlessly, he would charge straight into a herd. Guided by Makoons's knees and legs, the pony would follow the buffalo Makoons wished to hunt. The pony would run alongside the beast, cutting it away from the herd. Then it would run up alongside the buffalo. As soon as the shot resounded, it would veer away from the dangerous buffalo. The pony was being trained to keep a steady gait so that its rider could draw a bow or load a gun—a complicated procedure.

At first Whirlwind shied, prancing sideways, suspicious, as Makoons raced him toward the buffalo hide robe. Makoons allowed his pony to approach the hide, to look it over and smell it. Then he turned around and raced at the buffalo hide again. Each time he passed, the pony grew more accustomed to the dark, curly buffalo hide. When he was so confident that he completely ignored the hide, Animikiins tied a rope to the hide. As soon as Makoons rode the pony close, Animikiins set the hide moving.

The pony stopped so suddenly that Makoons nearly fell off. But they persisted until the pony lost its fear.

Once the pony fearlessly ran right toward and alongside the buffalo hide, Animikiins gave Makoons his bow so that he could draw it—or pretend to, since his arms were still weak after his illness. Animikiins also had a rifle, and he had to trade for the metal to make bullets. A buffalo hunter made his own bullets from lead that he melted over fire and poured into bullet molds. The hunter had to keep three or four lead bullets in his mouth. During the hunt, he would take a bullet out of his mouth, put it down the barrel with the correct amount of gunpowder, then use a ramrod to tamp the charge down tightly. All of this had to be done while riding a pony at breakneck speed! The bow and arrow was as accurate a piece of technology as the rifle, which had to be loaded for every shot, so many still used bows. Makoons went through the motions with the bow, then Animikiins handed him his musket, but didn't really load the gun. Makoons rode with pebbles instead of bullets in his mouth. The small stones wobbled and clicked against his teeth. It wasn't much fun. He spat them out and slowed his horse to a walk.

"Ginitam, your turn," said Makoons to Chickadee.

"Geget! I'm ready," said Chickadee.

Chickadee rode a spotted horse called Wing. This horse belonged to Uncle Quill, and it was used to chasing buffalo and anything else. It was a good horse—a big mare the color of dust, loyal of heart and steady. Chickadee got on and practiced with the bow, then a stick in his hand instead of his father's gun. Wing jumped forward eagerly, and Chickadee flew off her back.

He stood up and said "Gurk!" He had swallowed a pebble, but was too embarrassed to tell anyone. The other two pebbles he spat out. How did Makoons ride so well? He made it look easy.

"You flew like a bird." Animikiins smiled. "But don't worry. I fell off a lot when I first started."

He calmed down the horse and led her back to Chickadee. "Take your time, my boy! Don't be impatient. Get the feel of your horse. Don't yank her by the mane—hold her with your legs. Stick to her like a wood tick."

In moments, Chickadee again flew off, quick-feathered as his namesake. Wing stopped and waited for Chickadee to get back on this time. And so it went, Makoons and his horse fast as two whirling winds, darting back and forth. Wing and Chickadee like two birds flying opposite directions. Up and down.

At last Chickadee jolted to earth so hard he felt tears spurt from his eyes.

Makoons looked down at him, worried. Chickadee glared up at his brother.

"What are you looking at?"

"Gaawiin gegoo!" Makoons galloped off.

"Nothing?"

Chickadee hid the tears from his father and brother. Furious, he stomped away and slumped behind the little cabin on a big rock that jutted from the earth. There, in the shade, he wiped his face and breathed hard until his heart resumed its usual cheer. He heard his namesake, the chickadee, calling him from a nearby branch, telling him he was fine, he was doing well. Telling him not to give up.

"Miigwech, my little namesake," he said wearily.

He had learned always to listen to the chickadee.

He slapped the dirt off his pants and got back up. Walking around the side of the cabin, he stopped, amazed and envious, to watch Makoons galloping around and around the field, evading obstacles, sticking tight when Whirlwind jumped over a log. Makoons was laughing and shouting, oblivious of his father and brother. Chickadee walked up to his father and stood beside him. Animikiins was a lean man, with the same ferocious hawklike face he'd had as a boy, when Chickadee's mother, Omakayas, had met him. Animikiins had been angry and hungry then. Although hunger had come to stalk the little family many times, Animikiins had grown bighearted through desperation. He was a man of trustworthy kindness, and his hunting skills had many times rescued the family from disaster. Omakayas loved him dearly and made all of his clothing with great care. He wore deerskin pants with fringe and a beaded strip along the leg, a blue flowered cloth shirt, a small yellow feather tied in his hair, which was carefully oiled and braided by Chickadee's mother. The boys tried to evade her strict combing and braiding, but she was tenacious. Every morning she caught them and made them sit. She did not want others to see her men messy-headed—neatly braided hair was a sign someone cared for you.

"How does he ride so well?" Chickadee asked his father. "I thought when he got back on the horse he would wobble, the way he walks. He was so sick!"

"Maybe the horse gives him power," said Animikiins. "It has always been like this with your brother. You know that."

Animikiins was right. Makoons was a natural rider. Once on a horse he was so happy the horse sensed it and obeyed him. Chickadee liked to ride horses, but he didn't have the same connection somehow. He watched his brother weaving back and forth through the grass, evading imaginary buffalo. Makoons was still thin and frail-looking, but there was a wild exuberance in his eyes and laughing face. Chickadee longed to ride free with his brother, so he got back on the patient Wing and started slow, sticking like a wood tick. He decided he would not give up until he could ride with ease, no matter how many times he fell off.

After Quill watched Chickadee fall off for another hour, he winced, shook his head, and said to Animikiins that they'd better find him a shorter horse, a pony. It wouldn't be so far for him to fall! Wing was used to having Quill ride her. The perfect pony for Chickadee was just north of the camp, said Quill, and he set off to trade a buffalo robe and some blankets for it. Late in the day, he rode back with a wild fuzzy yellow pony that frothed furiously at the mouth and looked outraged at being tied behind Wing.

"Yours," said Quill grandly, handing the end of the rope halter to Chickadee.

The yellow pony reared, spooked, bucked, kicked up a storm of dust.

Chickadee was whipped side to side. The rope burned his palms. He tried not to yell with fear, but a strangled gurgle came out of his mouth. At last, Quill kindly took the rope out of Chickadee's terrified grip. The yellow pony went meek and trotted calmly behind Quill.

"What are you naming your horse?" asked Makoons.

"Mean Heart," said Chickadee. "Why does it follow Quill so nicely and then go crazy with me?"

"Name it something the opposite of how it behaves," advised Makoons.

Chickadee was very tired, but that thought made him grin. Just being around his twin lifted his spirits.

"How about Sweet? Wiishkob? Or Duckling? Zhiishiibens? Maybe Spirit Mouse? Or Happy Little Prancing Killer?"

Laughing, the twins thought of name after name.

"Zaagime, Mosquito!"

"Ninimoshehn!"

"That's the perfect name," laughed Chickadee. "Maybe if I call her Sweetheart, if she hears it every time I call, someday she'll break down and love me in return."

So that became the name of the little yellow horse. Ninimoshehn. Or just Ehn! when Chickadee was scared, tossed, or trying so hard to stay on that the whole name wouldn't come out of his mouth. Passing by the pasture where Chickadee practiced, his mother and grandmother heard him shouting, "Sweetheart, oh Sweetheart, oof, awrg, eiii! Owah! Sweetheart! Don't drop me! Slow down! Be nice, Sweetheart! Sweetheart, don't bite me! Sweetheart, no kicking! Ow! Let go of my shirt, Sweetheart! Wah!"

"What kind of boys are you raising?" said their grandmother Yellow Kettle with a severe look at Omakayas.

Nokomis began to laugh, and Omakayas grinned. Her grandmother had a burbling laugh that was contagious. Though twenty years younger, with fewer aches and pains,

Nokomis's daughter Yellow Kettle rarely even chuckled.

"Sweetheart, no kicking! Sweetheart, don't bite me!" Nokomis laughed. "Did you really think Chickadee was calling out to a girlfriend?"

Omakayas burst into laughter and she and Nokomis went on until their eyes teared and their stomachs ached. Yellow Kettle retained her dignity.

"Boys get in trouble very young these days," she sniffed. "It doesn't hurt to be suspicious."

# TWO

## STRANGE CREATURE

Each morning now, when Chickadee walked into the pasture, he rejected his brother's advice. Makoons had told him to bring his pony a treat—a bit of bannock, a handful of grass, something sweet—every single time he approached. But if a bit of maple sugar or honeycomb came his way, Chickadee had always eaten it all. The idea of saving even one bit for a horse seemed crazy! The yellow pony on the edge of the grass, tied to a stake, eyed Chickadee bitterly and pawed the earth. He was thirsty and hungry. All the grass within his reach was devoured. And now this useless human probably expected to jump on his back! Well, just let him try.

Chickadee did try, over and over.

At last Chickadee stopped, exhausted. Accepting his brother's advice, he hauled some water over in his mother's best kettle, and let the pony drink before his mother saw. He also picked some juicy grass. Makoons had told him that even if a horse had lots of grass it would like it better if you picked it.

Like magic, Sweetheart let him get on without a kick.

Chickadee quickly sneaked the kettle back and stole a tiny bit of bread from under a piece of cloth.

After that, he saved bits of bannock, picked armfuls of the sweetest grass, made certain that he had something his pony would like every single time he approached. His black and blue spots began to turn green, then yellow, then disappear. His aching eased. One day he came to the pasture, said "Sweetheart," and his pony pricked up her ears, trotted over to him, and put her soft chin on his shoulder. Chickadee stroked her in wonder. He got on to ride and this time he flowed with his pony, riding fast or slow. Sometimes another pony ran beside them just for fun. For the first time, as he rode, Chickadee found that he was smiling in joyous wonder. He was actually having fun.

As the days passed, Makoons and Chickadee found they walked in a new way—a little bowlegged. Makoons began to learn how to fire his father's hunting rifle while running full tilt ahead on Whirlwind. He still didn't use actual ammunition or gunpowder, for he was learning to maneuver while holding on firmly to his horse with his knees, steering through obstacles. Someday he would race alongside a real buffalo and pretend to fire while in motion. Day after day, he practiced this maneuver. Animikiins fired his gun off near the horse, teaching Whirlwind not to spook in fear. Finally, his father allowed Makoons to use real ammunition. For the first time he actually took a shot at a the target, which was nothing more than a leaf fixed to a piece of bark, about the height of a buffalo, and just behind the shoulder. He shot the leaf off the bark.

"Howah," said Animikiins softly.

Chickadee tried to smile, but all he could think was that he still had a very, very long way to go.

Everyone gathered for a feast of thanks—winter and spring had been times of hardship and fear, but the family was together now. The gracious sun stroked their shoulders, the wind was light, prairie roses budding, the horses happily devouring tender new grasses. The women had spent the afternoon in the shade plucking feathers, laughing and talking. A whole family's feast of duck was now cooking, boiling away in big pots above the coals of an open fire, and the boys were so hungry they could barely sit still.

Omakayas nodded toward the river, nearly half a mile away. She was cooking along with Zozie, who was the boys' adopted big sister and Omakayas's treasured daughter.

"The wood is low, my boys. Take your ropes."

Although their bellies pinched, Makoons and Chickadee grabbed the ropes they would use to bundle the dead wood they'd pick up along the river. They ran, for the delicious scent of cooking duck moved them powerfully. Chickadee slowed to keep pace with his faltering brother. Although he could ride with enormous skill, Makoons couldn't run very far. He was still struggling to find the balance and strength he had lost during sickness. He bent over once to catch his breath, dizzy, and from then on could only walk. Chickadee saw that his face had turned pale gray again, and he worried.

"Give me your rope, my brother. I'll get the wood and we can carry it back together. Don't run or you'll get sick again."

Makoons nodded and smiled at the ground. His whispered thanks was hardly audible to Chickadee, who ran lightly down to the Red River. There, he found a large washup of dry dead branches and broke them easily into carrying lengths. By the time Makoons reached the river, he'd made two bundles they could carry on their backs. But when Makoons hefted his bundle, the strain in his face was too much for Chickadee.

"I can take them both," he said.

Exhausted, Makoons trudged alongside his overburdened twin.

***

When they were in sight of the camp, their grandmother Yellow Kettle, saw them first. She was sitting with Nokomis, who was so old her hair glowed white and her clouded eyes reflected light. Nokomis had soft skin and a soft voice, except of course for her exuberant laugh. Nokomis was kindness through and through. She was very happy these days because a remarkable thing had occurred.

One day, Nokomis had admired the plantings of another old woman. This woman told her that a man named Albert LaPautre had sold her a bag of seeds.

Stunned, Nokomis told how LaPautre himself had stolen everything the family had owned back in Minnesota, including the seeds she had been saving ever since the family left their original home on Madeline Island. The woman had divided her garden seeds with Nokomis. With great joy, Nokomis accepted the seeds—old friends! These were the great-great-grandsons and -granddaughters of the seeds of the plants she'd nurtured so long ago in her gardens on Madeline Island. She recognized the varieties—the colored corns and blue potato eyes, the spotted beans, the delicate shapes of the thickly fleshed varieties of squash. Nokomis had been yearning to grow a garden once again, as she had many years before. Now she would have her original garden back.

Today, the family had worked until the earth was turned up, black and rich. Nokomis had planted her garden. Now Deydey, the husband of Yellow Kettle, grandfather of the twins, was carving the last touches on a cane for Nokomis. He was making garden tools for her as well, tying antlers to saplings, fixing a piece of bent metal into a hoe. He, too, had become kindlier with every passing year. But, true to herself, Yellow Kettle had grown ever more irritable with time. She'd always had a temper. It used to flare out of her and then disappear, but now it seemed she was always harboring a bed of dark red coals. She jumped up and hurried out to scold the boys as soon as she saw them.

"Why did you go down to the river, Makoons? You'll get sick again. And you, Chickadee, why did you let your brother go down to the river? What's wrong with you? He could have gotten all sick again. Do you want to kill him? Is that what you want?"

That's how she always talked—her tongue could

scorch. Chickadee was used to it. But how unfair! Yellow Kettle hustled Makoons toward the fire, patting his hands and scolding him all the harder. Chickadee scowled, even though the food smelled so good he almost shouted with joy. Here he was with two big loads of wood, expecting praise, and all he got was blame. But again, that was Yellow Kettle. Gitchi-Nokomis, his great-grandmother, peered at him as he came near the fire. She opened her eyes wide and said, "Howah! Look at my grandson! He carries enough wood for two strong boys! Enough to roast a whole flock of ducks!"

Deydey rose and tousled Chickadee's head. He helped pile the sticks when Chickadee dropped them to the ground. Deydey was restless in his old age and kept moving all day, which kept him strong. He never seemed angry or annoyed like Yellow Kettle, but he rarely spoke. Silence had settled deeper around him with every year. His great shoulders and powerful neck had dwindled, but his eyes were surprisingly sharp. Long ago, he had been treated with a special medicine for eyesight and Nokomis lamented that the tree she needed grew back in the woods and forest, where they had come from, and not here, on the great plains, where they made their new life.

Still, the medicine had worked well and his vision remained clear.

The boys' Auntie Angeline, her husband, Fishtail, and their adopted daughter, Opichi, or Robin, burst around the corner of the cabin. Opichi was like her namesake bird. She was a round, happy, sunny-faced girl with glossy braids and a ten-dency to sing. Just when her mother and father were convinced they would have no children because of Angeline's illness, smallpox, which 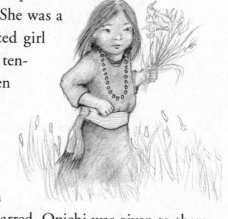 had left her lovely face scarred, Opichi was given to them to brighten the world. She had wandered into the camp, nobody knew from where. She was clearly Amishinaabe, but her origins were a mystery. Angeline and Fishtail had rushed to keep her.

"We are rich with food!" sang Opichi as they walked into camp.

She and her new parents had been out digging wild onions. Fishtail carried the sack, which was much too light for his strong arms. Opichi also carried a skin container made from buffalo rawhide—Omakayas had learned to make these containers the year before from a Metis, or a French and Ojibwe mixed-blood woman. Now that the family had left behind the great stands of birch trees, whose bark they'd used to make carrying baskets, they relied upon a new source—the buffalo. Opichi had filled her container with the eggs of ducks, cowbirds, prairie hens, coots, and other birds. These she brought to Yellow Kettle, for they were her favorite food. Yellow Kettle even preferred the eggs that contained the unhatched baby birds, and devoured them whole, smacking her lips. Yellow Kettle was fierce in everything, including what she ate. But the last person to enter the camp was fiercer yet.

Two Strike was a powerful, arrogant storm of a woman. She respected Omakayas's skills but had never been interested in cooking, gardening, making baskets, or beading. She didn't sew. She did not enjoy babies. Two Strike did as she pleased and was happy. She preferred to hunt, ride, shoot, and steal. Two Strike slept on the ground, lived in the open, washed when it rained, smelled like a wild animal when it didn't. She loved knives, and carried them on her person at all times. She had a knife in her legging, two knives at her waist, a knife on her arm in a special band. They were safely stowed in beaded knife sheaths that Omakayas made for her. The two women had grown up together and were fiercely loyal. Two Strike was the birth mother of the twins' older sister, Zozie. But the baby terrified Two Strike so badly that she'd thrust the infant into Omakayas's arms and fled the scene. If anyone remembered that Two Strike was a mother, they'd forgotten. The term just didn't fit.

Two Strike leapt off her alert brown horse. She tethered him and strode into the camp. Everybody looked up expectantly. You never knew what she'd say, never knew what she'd be carrying, never knew what she might have found or killed or stolen. Now, from underneath her coat, which lengthened to a sort of pants/dress sewn specifically for Two Strike's needs by Omakayas, she pulled something curly and pale. Everyone went silent. It was a creature. With uncharacteristic gentleness, she set it upon the earth. She wore an odd expression, a look nobody but Omakayas had ever seen before—it was a look of confused tenderness. Two Strike's massive hand stroked the curly hide and nudged the animal forward. It stepped toward the others on fixed, wobbly, tentative legs, and said, "Baa!"

"Maanishtaanishens!" exclaimed Gitchi-Nokomis. She had heard, and seen sheep long ago on their original home, Madeline Island. Those funny-looking curly animals had belonged to the missionary family on the island. Where had this one come from?

"I found it," said Two Strike with bashful tenderness. "The mother had died of eating arrow grass. The baby stood over it, making this beautiful strange music."

"Music?" Chickadee nudged Makoons. They looked wide-eyed at each other, trying to contain their laughter. They peered over at their mother, who was staring at Two Strike, mystified.

"Baa!" the lamb bawled again, more piteous and insistant.

Two Strike bent over it with a handful of shredded grass, and tried to feed it.

"The maanishtaanishens needs milk, not grass," said Nokomis.

Everyone was quiet with a sense of wonder at Two Strike's behavior. Disappointed, she dropped the grass from her hands. Frowning, she filled a piece of deerskin with water, poked a hole in the end, and pressed the water into the lamb's hungry mouth. Two Strike looked scared. She looked uncharacteristically confused. She had fended off the advances of many men, including two brothers whose horses she had stolen, but who had nevertheless pursued her for months with desperate pleas of love. Ferociously, she'd finally beaten them off. She hadn't wanted anyone near her but her dogs. But now she was behaving with tenderness toward this odd curly thing. She scowled hard at the family's two dogs, who skulked around the outskirts of the fire, looking ready to devour the lamb. Both dogs caught her deadly look, yipped, and disappeared. Two Strike's voice was harsh, and she often growled or even snarled for emphasis. Yet when she turned back to the lamb, there came from her lips a sound that could only be described as a croon.

"Unbelievable," Zozie whispered, shaking her head, hiding her smile. There was a bit of awed hurt in her face. Obviously, Two Strike couldn't feel this way about any human being, including her own daughter. Oh well. Zozie shrugged. She'd always been better off with Omakayas, whose nature it was to love children. She praised Zozie every day and told her that she was a wonderful daughter.

Animikiins adjusted the fire. Omakayas tested the birds, removed them from the pot, and put them onto the pieces of elm bark they used as plates. There were sixteen birds, enough with some left over for those who could eat two—that would include Uncle Quill, who now emerged from the grassy place he'd spread his blanket to rest after hunting.

Quill immediately reached for the food in his sister Omakayas's hand. What a brother! She spanked away his fingers. He was Quill. All his life he had grabbed food, usually straight from a hot stewpot. When Omakayas was a young girl, Quill had often snatched the food directly from her hand as she was about to eat it. So she was always prepared for his greedy, happy, snatching ways. Quill just shrugged and sat down, grinning with surprise at the lamb.

"Are we going to roast it tomorrow?" he asked Two Strike. He smacked his lips and rubbed his hands.

The look of utter loathing and rage that Two Strike turned upon him might have blasted a lesser man to dust. Quill just laughed. His laugh was so warm and affectionate that nobody (except Yellow Kettle) could hold a grudge or feel anger more than a moment with Quill. He could steal the very food from your fingers and still get smiles.

When everybody had their food, Nokomis blessed it with thanks to Gizhe Manidoo, the great kind spirit that moves and lives in all things. As soon as the words left her mouth, everyone dug in and then there was just the sound of satisfied eating. The dogs crept close again because they knew Uncle Quill and the boy twins would sneakily throw the bones to them immediately. Omakayas would scold them because she always collected the duck carcasses after they had devoured the meat and soupy broth, into which she put wild onions, potatoes, or wild rice. She collected them because Nokomis had taught her to return their bones to the water as a sign of respect, and also so that there would always be ducks.

"So tell us, Two Strike," said Quill, after he'd eaten the first duck on his plate, "where did you steal your curly little sweetheart?"

"I didn't steal him," said Two Strike in a voice with an undertone of surprised hurt. "I stole his mother. But she went and ate bad grass and died. She left me this clever little being."

She tickled the lamb under the chin, but in desperation it took her finger in its mouth and tried to get some milk out of it.

"Poor little thing," said Angeline. "Let's bring it to Fly."

29

Fly was a mare who belonged to Angeline and Fishtail. The poor mother was moping because her most recent foal had died. She was a spotted roan, a very unusual and beautiful horse, and she was much beloved by the couple. She was so gentle that even Opichi could ride her.

"Maybe Fly will nurse this lamb. Maybe it would make her happy."

"I would be so grateful," said Two Strike seriously. Her voice choked up a little. She had been attempting to feed the lamb some cooked duck.

Angeline and Fishtail looked at each other, biting their lips and trying hard to stay as serious as Two Strike. They had never seen such behavior in their wild friend. They were determined to save the cause, the lamb.

They went off to the horse pasture—Two Strike carried the lamb, and Opichi rambled merrily beside her.

"If only Fly will adopt my little being," said Two Strike gently, stroking the lamb's head.

"She will," said Opichi sympathetically, holding the tiny hoof.

They followed Angeline and Fishtail, who had an idea. Before they got to the pasture, Angeline nodded at Fishtail. When the foal had died, he'd taken its skin and stretched it out, anchored by stones. He had put it out to dry on a scaffold, out of reach of the dogs. Now he took it down, flopped it like a sad limp shirt over his arm, and walked beside them to the pasture.

Quill had created an interesting brush fence for the animals—it was concocted of every sort of barrier he could find, from driftwood to balled-up roots and weeds, to fence rails abandoned by settlers whose farms had failed. To get into the pasture, he had a real gate that he'd found on the riverbank. It must have drifted off in some flood, from some forgotten house somewhere, built too close to its banks—it was a beautiful gate and Quill was proud of it.

Fishtail ceremoniously opened the gate and whistled to Fly. She was standing on the other side of the pasture. When she heard the whistle, she flicked back an ear and slowly turned with mournful eyes. She stared at them as if reproaching them for disturbing her unhappy meditations. With a sigh, she plodded over to them, head held low.

Angeline stepped up beside Fly, stroked her neck, and scratched gently behind her ears. Fly was especially sensitive in her loss. Suddenly, her head jerked around. She smelled her baby. Fishtail had draped and tied the foal's hide around the lamb, and with quick dexterity put the lamb to her aching, swollen teat. Instantly, the lamb began to nurse. Angeline stepped back as Fly's eyes bulged. The sad mare bent around to put her soft nose to the lamb. She knew something was not right. She pulled away, suspicious. But the lamb trotted forward, nuzzled her, insisted on nursing. Fly stared in consternation. She looked at the humans, at Two Strike, who stood by anxiously, wringing her hands. Fly's expression was almost comical. What is

31

*happening,* she seemed to say with her shocked eyes, startled ears and flaring velvet nostrils. She took a final look, down, at the sinister baby. Oh well, she seemed to shrug. Then she put her head down to crop grass as the lamb drank and drank.

Two Strike almost strangled Fishtail with her hug. Angeline grabbed Opichi and they stepped out of reach. Two Strike's hug was always bumpy with hidden knives.

# THREE

# THE SIGHTING

After the meal Nokomis burned the bark plates and stirred the kettle of leftovers that would make tomorrow's soup. Although she was ancient, with hair so white and wispy the sun shone through like the seed head of a dandelion, she enjoyed any work that she could do—and she did it with great calm and cheer. As for Yellow Kettle, she worked hard too, but as she worked she usually talked to herself, chewing over things that people did wrong, hissing her outrage. As she sewed a new pair of pants for Uncle Quill, her grown son, she muttered.

"He just never grows up, never grows up. Still acts like a crazy boy. Look how he rips his pants up. And he had a woman who fixed things for him but she left him. Now he's alone. What woman would want such a bad boy, that's what he was, bad! Now his mischief got him into trouble. Never listened to me! I told him! I told him!"

While she was sewing beside the fire, the evening had grown cool. As she talked, Quill stole up behind her. He grabbed a little stick off the ground and touched her head.

"Wha! These flies!" She whacked at her head.

Quill touched her head gently on the side with the stick.

"Aagh!"

Yellow Kettle whipped the pants around her head.

Quill touched her back. She slapped her back. Her elbow. She scratched her elbow. He was enjoying his game enormously by the time Omakayas came and put a stop to it. She grabbed the stick out of his hand.

"Will you never grow up?"

"Why should I?" he cried, yelping in mock injury. "And how can I grow up when all of my women relatives treat me like a child!"

He ran to look after his horse. He loved Wing, and he loved his Red River oxcart. He had made it himself, every bit, learned from an expert at oxcarts. There wasn't one piece of metal used in its construction. He could fix it by stopping near a tree and using hand tools to create a new part. During the summer, he parked his oxcart and lived beneath it. When there were too many mosquitoes, he surrounded himself with fires. When it rained, he put blankets up on the sides of the cart and slept beneath. His wife had tried to tame him, to make him live indoors and do things properly. Quill had refused. She couldn't throw him out of the house, because he wouldn't live in one. But she did toss him out of her life. Now he sat outside on a little chair he'd carved from a stump and smoked his pipe, gazing out into the distance. Soon he'd take down the two blankets that had been airing on top of the cart. He felt the luxury of two blankets, one to fold beneath his body, the other to cover him against the dew. He had an arm for a pillow. What else could a man need? Soft puffs of smoke wound into the dusky shadows.

Well, there was one thing a man might need.

"A new wife," he said softly.

Passing behind him, Yellow Kettle heard.

"A new wife," she scoffed. "You'll never get one! You're trouble!"

Quill looked after his mother as she walked away and thought that if she could find a husband in her life, then he could surely find a wife. For if anyone was trouble, it was Yellow Kettle. He had inherited her will, her energy, but, fortunately, not her anger. He smiled indulgently. After all, her scolding was only noise, and as she passed she had tossed his pair of mended pants at his head.

Over the next few days, the camp was noisy with new people arriving. To get away, Makoons and Chickadee rode their horses down to the river where it meandered into an oxbow. They tied up their horses and let them graze while they caught fish—golden eyes and fat, slow catfish. A snapping turtle surfaced and watched them with a hooded gaze until Chickadee threw a rock at it.

"Brother," said Makoons, "don't offend that old grandfather. You could ruin our luck."

"He's robbing our lines, more like it." Chickadee hoisted a line with half a fish snapped neatly off.

"After your insult," said Makoons, "you'll be lucky to get half a fish."

Makoons was wrong, however. The old grandfather must have thought them beneath his notice. They caught a string of fish and rode back to their mother. She admired the size of the fish. They ate some of her duck stew and then hopped back on the horses to roam the low hills outside of Pembina that afternoon, checking rabbit snares. They climbed the highest hill they could find, which wasn't really very high, but from that place they could see west, far out onto the plains, a world of waving grass.

As they sat on their horses in the sweeping wind, they could see forever. From one side of the world a storm moved away with dark nets of rain on the horizon. From the other side of the world a set of buoyant clouds bounced along in hot sunshine. Banks of geese and dark flocks of duck rose and fell against these clouds. Other birds wheeled and roamed the air. The air was loud with gurgling larks and the trills of blackbirds. Violently blue buntings popped up here and there in the grass.
Tiny flashes of finch and
hummingbird, clouds
of hunting dragonflies,
the shadows of cranes,
eagles, hawks—it was a twitch-
ing, fluttering, darting vision of
birds and grass.

"Nashke," said Chickadee slowly, raising his chin, squinting at the sunny side of the world. "What is that?"

The emphatic line of the horizon wavered and moved, but it was not a heat mirage. There was no shimmering quality. It was something else. They breathed in, slowly, hoping it was what they thought it might be. They waited, blinking, shadowing their faces, willing themselves not to say it until they made sure. Finally, they looked at each other, nodded, and grinned.

"Mashkode-bizhikiwag," they said at the same time.

With a swift motion they turned and rode, hard and fast as they could, back to camp.

# FOUR

# BUFFALO!

The twins rode into camp like a double tornado. Buffalo!
Their small family cabin was surrounded by skin tents,
bark huts, family and friends who had returned to Pembina
during the summer. Most of them were relatives and fol-
lowers of Chief Little Shell. The family already knew and
got along with all of them except a hunter nicknamed Gichi
Noodin, Big Wind. He was conceited, always puffing out
his chest and bragging of his exploits to anyone who would
listen. From each small dwelling a person or two spilled out
yelling in excitement. Gichi Noodin jumped onto a small
rock, the better to be seen. He wore a tight skin under-
shirt so that his muscles were visible for easy admiration.

He threw back his head, let the wind whip his gleaming, streaming hair, and flexed his muscles, for he was truly big and strong. He was hoping women watched him, and he was known to be very jealous of the leader, Little Shell. Little Shell ignored him and prepared his hunting horse and rifle. With a sideways glance at the chief's preparations, Gichi Noodin jumped off his rock and scrambled to throw his gear together. He wanted to be the first scout on the scene.

At the edge of the trampled grass, Uncle Quill napped underneath his oxcart with his hat flopped over his face. Farther on, staked in the tall grasses, buffalo ponies nickered and pricked up their ears. Wing, taller and more powerful than the others, yanked at her stake so hard she pulled it loose. Excitedly, she trotted to Quill, who was still snoring in spite of the chaos. The horse poked her nose underneath the cart's box and flipped the hat off the man's face. Quill chuckled in his sleep and clumsily batted at the horse's velvety muzzle.

"Oh, stop it, honey girl!" Quill made kissing noises but kept brushing his dream sweetheart's hand away from his cheeks and chin.

The horse grabbed a hank of the man's hair in its teeth and pulled.

"Aaaagh! Owey! Booni'ishin!"

Meanwhile, Makoons and Chickadee jumped off their horses and zigzagged through the family and friends, who were already making feverish preparations for the hunt. Makoons grabbed his uncle's shirt and yelled excitedly into his uncle's face. "Uncle! Uncle Quill! Buffalo!" Quill's eyes opened wide and he rolled out from underneath the oxcart. From inside the cart he pulled a piece of leather, which he threw onto Wings's back and cinched tight. He grabbed his rifle from a watertight rawhide container tethered under the cart.

While Quill was pulling himself together, slurping water from a dipper that his mother, old Yellow Kettle, carried around the camp, Makoons ran into the grass. He quickly retrieved Whirlwind, who tossed his head high in glee. Holding his pony's rope halter, Makoons led it to a stream. As the pony drank, Makoons swung himself back up. He was going to scout the herd with the grown-ups, whether they wanted him or not.

"Stay here," said Animikiins sternly to his sons. Then he whirled on his horse and galloped away. Chickadee went to help his mother ready the camp to move behind the hunt.

Little Shell rode off without speaking.

Gichi Noodin looked down at Makoons disdainfully. Next to him, Two Strike busied herself.

"Stay home, little girls," Gichi Noodin said to them both.

Little girls? Two Strike heard him and fury lighted in her eye. She vaulted onto her horse.

"Little girl?" she cried. "I am a bigger woman than you are a man!"

As she raced past Gichi Noodin, she leaned over and gave him a massive push. With a strangled squawk of surprise, Gichi Noodin vanished over the side of his horse. The horse had hated Gichi Noodin's fancy spurs and rough ways. Now it pranced away, stopping to snatch mouthfuls of grass. Gichi Noodin rose from the ground and gazed in shock after the bold woman, Two Strike, now out of reach. Turning back to his horse, he tried to catch it. But his horse seemed to think it was fun to let Gichi Noodin get close and then bolt just when the man thought he was in reach.

"You stay put!" shouted Quill over his shoulder to Makoons, but he was laughing so hard at Gichi Noodin that there wasn't much conviction in his voice. Makoons decided to follow Quill and Two Strike.

"Come back!" cried Omakayas, chasing after her son.

"Stop, brother," yelled Chickadee.

It was too late. Makoons was already following the scouting party toward the herd of buffalo. Left behind, Chickadee hopped around in frustration. He wanted to go too. But he couldn't catch Sweetheart, no matter how fast he ran or how longingly he cried out his horse's name. Still, he was not alone with this horse-catching problem. After a few fruitless minutes Chickadee quit trying because the sight of Gichi Noodin was so entertaining. The big strapping man with the flowing hair had donned a beautiful shirt. But he made a foolish leap toward his horse, and fell in a patch of mud. His snow-white shirt, which was tight-sleeved to show his manly biceps and thrilling chest, had not only split down the side but its fetching whiteness was spoiled with dirt. Gichi Noodin screamed at his horse and threw clumps of mud.

Makoons rode in a direct line behind the scouts and stayed just far enough back. They couldn't see him with one glance over their shoulders. No, they would have to turn all the way around on their saddles, but they didn't do that. They were so excited about the buffalo that they bolted ahead to the rise from which the boys had told them they'd spotted the herd. When nearly there, Two Strike and the men slowed their horses to a walk. Then they dismounted and sneaked forward. Makoons did too. He came up behind his uncles and father so quietly that they didn't notice him, or so Makoons thought. The men, with Makoons among them, stooped down, level with the grasses, staring fixedly at the horizon.

After a time, Quill said quietly, "Those boys have sharp eyes. Too bad Makoons is so foolhardy and disobedient."

"Buffalo hunting rules are strict," growled Two Strike.

Behind them, Makoons gulped and said nothing.

"Good thing he didn't follow us," said Animikiins.

"If he followed us, we'd have to whip him for sure," added Fishtail.

"If he wants to be a man, he must stand a man's punishment," said Little Shell.

There was silence. Only the wind sighed in the grass. Step by step Makoons backed away, drawing Whirlwind with him until he dared slip onto his pony's back. Makoons then made a mad dash for home, staked Whirlwind in the grass, and sneaked up beside Chickadee, who had left off trying to catch his pony entirely. Chickadee was surprised by his brother's stealth.

"Something brought you back fast!"

"They spoke of whipping me."

"Good thing you disappeared. Look, let's work together. Pretend you were always here. Come on, let's get the packs ready, sharpen the skinning knives. Take down the drying racks, huh? Nokomis will like that. She'll feed us good if we bundle up the drying racks and tie them behind the dogs!"

Makoons took a bit of bannock from his pocket and lured a big sad-eyed hungry-looking gray dog over. He harnessed up a travois—two long poles, a harness. Then he tied on as large a bundle of sticks as the dog could manage. As soon as the travois was hooked up, the dog looked more cheerful. Camp dogs knew when there was a buffalo hunt. They were eager to help when they knew they would be fed. Chickadee harnessed another dog— big-eared, cheerful, and honey-brown—and they loaded this dog's travois with firewood. Omakayas saw her twin boys, praised them, and captured another dog with hand-outs. This dog was honored with the task of dragging her best kettle. Angeline had already attached poles and a carrying sling to her horse. She hoisted Opichi onto Fly and put the halter in her daughter's chubby hands. Angeline trusted her horse not to move too quickly with a child riding—she had trained Fly with great care. The lovely spotted roan stayed steady even though a palpable excitement roiled the camp, and from time to time she reached down affectionately to nuzzle her curly, hopping, strangely alien but playful little foal.

Soon the scouts arrived back in the camp.

Animikiins and Little Shell would be the buffalo chiefs. They had done well in every hunt.

"Be certain to follow the buffalo chiefs," the scouts warned. "Obey everything and the hunt will go well. Above all, do not shoot until they give the signal. Do not startle the herd."

Gichi Noodin finally caught his horse and mounted up. When he heard the scouts, he glowered with jealousy and smoothed his second-best shirt across his manly chest. He tied his hair back with a bright cloth and polished his hunting gun. The other hunters looked like a ragtag bunch beside him, but they were determined to provide for their families. The buffalo they shot would be used entirely— from hoof to horn. They gathered, holding their rifles in one hand, pouches of shot and gunpowder in the other. About a third of the men, including Fishtail and Animikiins, carried bows and quivers of arrows. Theirs were made by Deydey, and were superior weapons. Hunting rifles or old muskets could misfire. Some of the hunters had special repeating rifles though, recently invented. Little Shell had such a rifle, which had been given to him during the treaty negotiations. It was admired by many people. Uncle Quill, who traded furs in the cities of St. Paul and Minneapolis, had a brand-new rifle as well. It did not need to be reloaded while riding on a horse. All of the hunters kept a few ready in their mouths. Those with the older rifles kept their gunpowder in hollow horns capped with rawhide. Many had ramrods on rawhide thongs around their necks, as well. They were ready for action. They had shed jackets, hats, packrolls, anything extra that might get in the way of hunting.

Before the hunting party started after the buffalo, Little Shell filled his pipe and passed it around the circle. Little Shell and Animikiins prayed on behalf of the generous buffalo and the generous spirit that moves and lives in all things, Gizhe Manidoo.

Nokomis stayed home, at the little cabin. Deydey would stay behind too, though Yellow Knife would go on. He would keep the cabin safe and help Nokomis work in the garden. Nokomis had planted her seeds and was watching them sprout. Not even a buffalo hunt could draw her from her garden—this time of watching was crucial. Deydey joked that she would probably sleep outside next to her baby plants.

"I would!" cried Nokomis. "If the zaagimeg would let me! They bite too hard!"

She had begun a fence of sticks, and was working it together to keep out any stray creature that might covet what was, to her, a magic replacement of her old happy world. For the rest of the family, of course, the garden was also going to be a crucial source of food. They had all helped plant the corn, especially, with expectant hope. Omakayas remembered guarding cornfields in their old, lost home. Yellow Kettle recalled making marvelous corn soups. And the potatoes, thought Angeline, would go very well with the bison her husband, Fishtail, would bring down in the hunt!

The hunters rode off in high spirits with the rest of the camp, except for Deydey and Nokomis, traveling behind. Although excited, Quill had also stayed behind long enough to harness his ox to his oxcart. The slow-moving train of dogs, children, pack-laden horses—everybody but the hunters themselves—would get to the scene of the buffalo hunt just in time to do the skinning, meat drying, the work of making a long-lasting food called pemmican, and even some smoking and tanning of hides if they camped long enough. Makoons and Chickadee had visions of sneaking away, in spite of the consequences, and joining

the hunt. Even though they knew the punishment for ruin-
ing a buffalo hunt could be severe, they were sure they'd
help and even become heroes.

"After all, we're the ones who discovered the herd!" said
Makoons.

"Geget, you are right," said Chickadee. He knew how
deeply his brother longed to use his training in a mighty
hunting charge.

"We can still sneak after them," said Makoons.

"I've got something better for you to do," said Quill,
who'd overheard them. "Why don't you drive my oxcart?"

Makoons and Chickadee jumped in excitement. Uncle
Quill had never allowed them to take the cart before.
Driving an oxcart was almost as good as being in the hunt!
They let Zozie use their horses as pack animals. Then they
set about imitating Quill, calling his sleepy ox and urging
it to follow the rest of the moving camp.

The camp moved inexorably ahead. Finally the last
horse and dog were passing from view. Chickadee and
Makoons, on the oxcart, were standing still in the dust the
camp left behind them, wondering how their uncle managed to get his ox moving.

"Haii!" yelled Chickadee.

"Howah!" yelled Makoons.

"Here we go!"

But nothing happened.

Chickadee had the reins first—they were taking turns.

He slapped the ox's back. That seemed to put it to sleep.

"Just wait," said Makoons. "He won't want to be left behind. Watch and see!"

Makoons was right. The drowsy ox opened his eyes and looked around. Nobody there. He could see the other oxen and horses moving ahead. Anxiously, he jolted into a walk. The ox just needed to follow the crowd and didn't like to feel alone.

They did have some other consolation, too. On the next hunt after this one, Animikiins had promised, they could bring their horses and ride along. They would not use weapons; they would not hunt. This was the next part of training. Their ponies would follow the other horses, and do as they did with no fear. They were animals of the herd, and copied their brothers and sisters.

"Next hunt," said Makoons to Whirlwind, "you'll be with the big horses!"

"Next hunt!" said Chickadee.

Meanwhile, the band of hunters raced quickly to the rise where the buffalo had been spotted, then stopped. Across a wide expanse of grassland, the herd still peacefully grazed. The hunters breathed sighs of relief, smiled in satisfaction. The buffalo could have started a run while they were gone or disappeared in any number of ways. Buffalo were a strange and unpredictable creature. Sometimes they didn't care who approached them and would stand still and watch a man walk right up to them. At other times the merest whiff of human scent would send them stampeding.

Today the humans were in luck. The wind was blowing toward the hunters, which meant it would not bring their scent to any skittish buffalo. Slowly, the hunters walked their horses down the rise. Carefully, the hunters walked their horses in the direction of the buffalo. It would just take one quick movement, sometimes, to startle the herd, and they wanted to make sure that they didn't make the buffalo start running from a great distance. They could lose the buffalo entirely into, say, Dakota country, to other hunters, or the animals might just spread out and dwindle away. Sometimes a herd mysteriously seemed to evaporate into the landscape. Most times, the hunters would just have a lot more work chasing the buffalo down and hunting them once they were spooked.

So the beginning of a buffalo hunt always started with a slow and cautious, even gentle sort of herding. As they moved toward the buffalo, seemingly without purpose, the buffalo continued to graze. Some of the great beasts had created wallows and stood in line to use them. The first buffalo, hot and harassed by flies, would gouge a hole in a moist spot and paw up the earth until it was muddy and cool. Then the buffalo would lie down and move in a circle, rolling on its back to get the full enjoyment of the mud, cooling off. When it finally rose, another buffalo would take its place. Here and there, they lined up one after the other to enjoy a particularly good wallow. By the next season, their wallow, with the mud stirred up and plenty of fertilizer from the buffalo, would stay strikingly green and round. These circles dotted the vast plains.

Closer, closer, the hunters walked their horses. The buffalo still hadn't noticed them. Great, shaggy, magnificent, dark, the beasts thrust the panting engines of their faces forward and devoured the steaming grass. They were the lords of the Great Plains, the keepers of its generous spirit, and their abundance made other life possible. They moved slowly away from something that they dimly sensed behind them, but they were not alarmed. It was a lazy day, an easy day, and the buffalo had no intention of doing anything but filling their bellies. The bulls hadn't started to fight over the cows yet. The orange-brown calves were just old enough to run beside their mothers. The new grass was thick and tender. Each animal had one or two brown birds that sat companionably upon the massive hump of its shoulders, or at that sensitive place right at the tail. The buffalo birds never went hungry, for the buffalo were end-less sources of ticks and flies. If the birds could have built their nests between the buffalo's horns or in their curly hump hides, they would have, but there was just no way to predict when a buffalo might want to take a nap or just roll over—for the joy of it.

The hunters sped up a little, but still the buffalo did not scare. Maybe the fine weather and gentle wind lulled them. Suddenly, the hunters were so close that they could clearly see every detail of the animals—the matted ends of their switching tails, their densely furred humps, their dark liquid eyes rolling in surprise.

"Now!"

Animikiins and Little Shell gave the signal. But Gichi Noodin had already started shooting. He had directly dis-obeyed the order. The consequences would come later. The herd stampeded, but the hunters were very close.

When a herd of buffalo breaks into a full-out run, the sound is deafening, a steady rolling thunder. Not only the sound, but the motion of such powerful mas-sive bodies hurtling through the air is terrifying. The big bulls with their heavy heads and necks ran hard. So did the reddish calves, sticking to their mothers tight in fear, charging along with the herd fast as they could on new legs. The hunters did not kill the tough old bulls, nor did they hunt the pregnant mothers or those with nursing calves.

Two Strike spotted the buffalo she wanted and her eager brown horse fearlessly cut it from the herd. Expertly, she rode beside. Just as she shot, the pony veered away, taking Two Strike out of danger. The buffalo took one big jump and died before it hit the ground. Animikiins killed two more. Fishtail missed his first but killed several others. Quill brought down four buffalo with his new rifle. Two Strike killed another. Then the herd outran them and vanished into the horizon where they had come from. Little Shell and his men, including Gichi Noodin, returned to the animals they'd killed and claimed.

When all of the hunters were together, they dismounted. Little Shell prayed and put tobacco on the ground. Then there was an uncomfortable silence.

"Gichi Noodin," said Animikiins. "You showed disrespect."

"Huh?" Gichi Noodin feigning shock. "Me?"

"You did not wait for the signal," said Little Shell. "Our families are lucky you did not cost us this hunt."

"I thought you gave the signal," said Gichi Noodin. His face was insolent, but his words were solemn. He shrugged. He pretended to be surprised and sorry, but it was obvious he was just trying to humor Little Shell.

"Watch it," said Two Strike.

"Oh, I'm watching," said Gichi Noodin, puffing out his chest and batting his long eyelashes at her. "My eyes are on *you*."

Two Strike's hands flashed to her knives, but Quill stopped her.

"Let's not have trouble," he said. "We had a good hunt here. Nashke! Look!"

Quill darted a hard look at Gichi Noodin, opened his arms and gestured around them.

Nearly thirty buffalo had been killed. There was food for everyone, a feast. There were hides to tan and robes to sell. They had bounty—horns for carrying gunpowder. Horns to carve into spoons. Bone to make the handles of knives, shoulder blades for hoes, sinew for sewing—on and on the list went. Most important, there was food. They would feast. The leftover meat would be pemmican. Good traveling food. The hunters started skinning the animals and soon the carts and horses from the camp began to arrive.

# FIVE

# THE GENEROUS ONES

T he families scattered and began to work, fast. They had to slice the hides off the buffalo. That would cool off the carcasses so that the meat would not spoil. This had to be quick work—there would be no stopping until it was completed. They were lucky to have killed the buffalo not far from a stream that wound lazily between sloughs. It would dry up by midsummer, but the water was very useful now. It meant they would be able to boil the best parts of the meat and render fat off the bones.

The hunters identified the buffalo that they had killed. "Of course, I killed the most," boasted Gichi Noodin. But it turned out he claimed two buffalo that the other hunters had seen Little Shell kill. Gichi Noodin pouted. Taking a dignified and hurt posture, he set to work. He was very slow because he was careful not to get blood on his pants or shirt. Also, he kept stepping back to admire his work and to see if anyone else was admiring him. Angeline and Opichi worked with Fishtail on the buffalo he had killed. Omakayas, Zozie, and Yellow Kettle began on the buffalo that Animikiins had brought down. Uncle Quill worked alongside Two Strike. She called the twins over and gave them each one of her razor-sharp knives so that they could learn how she took off the hide.

If the buffalo had been killed in winter, Two Strike would have started cutting at the belly in order to remove the hide whole and either sell it or use it as a warm robe for herself. But as it was early summer and the bison coats were thin and scroungy, Two Strike started her cut at the back to get at the tenderest meat. She would save the hide, but in pieces that she hoped Omakayas and Zozie would tan for her. Maybe they'd make her help tan those hides, she thought with a shudder, but she would try to get out of it! Perhaps she could bribe them or work on their sympathies. Two Strike hated tanning hides even more than they did, but at least she could press her twin nephews into work.

The twins helped Two Strike remove the hide down to the legs. Using short, quick strokes, they cut swiftly at the blue-white connecting membrane that lay under the hide. They cut away the hide just over the golden fat and still-warm meat. As they took off the hide, the meat swiftly cooled. There was a stiff wind, which kept the flies from settling. Still, during lulls in the breeze the flies buzzed madly around the entire scene, which was, no getting around it, a bloody sight of rampant butchery.

Here a leg, there a head, an entire hide, or the inner organs were being carried out of steaming collapsed carcasses. The smaller children were set to work collecting old, dried-out circles of buffalo dung, which littered the grass. The dung was used as fuel for fires. Once the meat was cut into thin strips, it would be draped across those drying racks that the dogs had carried to the kill. The buffalo provided the fuel for fires that smoked their own meat. They gave their brains, fat, and liver to be used in tanning their own hides. They provided tools with their bones that could be sharpened and used to flesh their carcasses. All winter, they had kept their killers warm and snug under curly robes. Indeed, as Little Shell had said in his prayer, the buffalo were a most generous animal.

The day went on and on, with a break here and there to replenish energy. Omakayas made certain that Makoons and Chickadee were given the nourishing marrow from bones that she cracked open with her pounding rock. The boys drank water, ate fresh buffalo bone marrow, and returned to their work. The sunlight shifted to shadow and the air cooled. Darkness crept from the grass and the women built the fires higher. Around the edges of the kill, just out of bow or gunshot range, the white wolves of the great plains glided. Watching. Waiting. Closer into the circle, the wolvish gray tame dogs waited also, and watched. They ate the gristle, they fought over the guts, they snapped up the bits of fat or meat that slipped unnoticed into the grass. All the people were tired, but there was no stopping until each carcass had been cut up and hauled to camp in pieces to be guarded. Little Shell commanded that the great heads of the killed buffalo be placed on a small hill that looked west, where the rest of the herd had disappeared. As the night deepened, Two Strike gave the twins a break.

"Don't wander off," she said. "I might need you."

The boys staggered a short way off, exhausted, and fell into some grass near the stream, where a copse of willow trembled in the cool breezes. They drank some water, but they weren't hungry. The buffalo marrow had filled them up. As they lay stretched out in the grass, nearly napping, they heard something odd. Something breathing.

"Do you hear that?" said Makoons.

"Where's it coming from?" Chickadee wondered.

The two boys turned over and crept through the grass toward the small, even, wheezing sound. Suddenly, it stopped. Makoons had the distinct feeling that if he parted the grass he would see *it*. Whatever it was. A wolf? Wolves were wary. A bear? Bears were wary. An enemy? Makoons was suddenly very afraid.

"Could be an enemy scouting us," he whispered to Chickadee.

Both of the boys went dead silent for a long time and did not move. The wheezing sound was not human, though, they decided. It was a scared little sound and stopped if they tried to move. Whatever was behind the grass, whatever *it* was, was afraid of them. So carefully they parted the grass.

Behind the strands, in the moonlight with its head stuffed as deeply in the base of the grass as it could go, there was a fuzzy red buffalo calf.

Its eyes were squeezed shut.

"It is hiding!"

"It thinks if he can't see us . . ."

". . . then we don't see him!"

Makoons and Chickadee were struck with pity.

Slowly, gently, they put their hands on the calf and began to stroke its baby fur. As they petted the calf, it lifted a mournful, bewildered face and blinked at them.

"We'll take care of you," said Makoons.

"Don't worry, you can belong to us," said Chickadee.

They put out their hands and the calf immediately, desperately, began to suck on their fingers. Makoons slipped off the rope that held up his pants, putting it around the calf's neck. With one hand holding up his pants and the other on the calf, he walked the little creature back to the camp. Chickadee held on too. They were sure that the calf would try to run away when he beheld the terrible sights of his buffalo people dead and destroyed. But the calf just stayed with them and did not seem to recognize his people all cut up so strangely into pieces. He didn't seem to feel any sadness or danger. Omakayas saw her sons with the calf and nudged Zozie. They stood up and couldn't help but laugh at the sight. As the boys walked the calf along, it seemed happy to be with them, like a big red dog. Opichi ran to the calf and stroked it with her short, chubby, blood-bathed hands. The calf didn't mind.

"We'd better make Makoons a new belt out of a piece of hide," said Omakayas. She began to cut away at the side of a skin.

"What are you going to do with it?" Zozie asked Omakayas.

"We're bringing him to Fly," said Makoons.

"Poor Fly," said Yellow Kettle. She had retained her grumpy attitude through a day of exhausting work. "Poor horse. You'll wear her out. And on a buffalo calf! We should kill it and skin it. I could use that soft hide for a tobacco pouch."

Makoons looked at her in horror, and Chickadee yelped a little to coax the calf away from his bloodthirsty grand-mother.

Staked in the grass, Fly was grazing, closely followed by Two Strike's lamb. The hungry calf trotted up to Fly and knew exactly what to do. Fly snorted, threw her head around, and stared in shocked disgust at her new baby. First that curly thing! Now this square-headed thing! My, she seemed to think, my babies are ugly! The calf was just old enough to chew grass, but needed to be with a mother. Right there, it adopted Fly by affectionately banging its head against her. What is happening now? her eyes seemed to say. Then she shrugged and settled back into eating, as if to say, Well, I love them anyway. From now on, it would be a battle for Fly's attention between the buffalo calf and the lamb. They weren't very good at taking turns.

From time to time the families dropped in the grass to rest, then rose again to continue working. The cool air revived them. The buffalo tongues, a delicacy, were cooked in Omakayas's kettle and given first to the elders and those honored for their hunting. Next the hump meat was cooked into a soup all could share. Two Strike lighted fire after fire to ring the camp with light. The wolves edged closer, howling with hunger and anticipation. The dogs barked at them. Fishtail fired his gun and they moved off to wait with steady patience.

As others worked, Quill dug a large deep hole. At the bottom of the hole he placed rocks. On top of the rocks he put down plenty of wood hauled from the side of the stream. He started the wood on fire, then let the fire in the pit burn to coals, heating the rocks underneath to a glowing red. While that was happening, he wove stream-willow wands into a great loose basket that held his favorite cuts of buffalo. He put the buffalo meat in the hole, covered it with a scraped hide, and then shoveled down dirt until the hide, the meat, the willow, the coals and the red hot rocks were buried. Overnight the buffalo cooked to a savory deliciousness. Just before dawn, he started digging up the buffalo meat, and as it was uncovered a scrumptious steam escaped, waking the entire camp.

Some people were sleeping, some still working. They had continued in shifts all through the night. The wolves had silently finished off the carcasses farthest from the camp and the vultures had descended to the little hill where the buffalo heads looked west. By next year, those skulls would lie there bleaching in the sun.

Makoons and Chickadee had slept hard, curled together on a soft robe from a previous hunt. They came to, groggily, awakened by the scent of cooked meat wafting from Quill's earth oven.

They ran first to their calf. He was curled up with the lamb. As soon as they were disturbed, the calf and the lamb jumped up and started butting heads. Fly dozed on her feet above them. So the boys ran back to help Quill.

Using antlers tied to the end of long sticks as their pitchforks, Quill and Two Strike lifted the basket of meat out onto flat rocks. Before returning to the rest of the work, everyone in the camp feasted. The meat was sweet, tender, and seasoned by the willow and by precious salt that Quill bought in St. Paul or traded for along the way.

Little Shell smacked his lips and asked for more. Animikiins and Fishtail couldn't get enough. Omakayas said that she was jealous of her brother's cooking talents. Makoons and Chickadee ate fast, filling their bellies until they couldn't eat another bite.

"My son has surprising skills," declared Yellow Kettle in an unusual fit of contentment. Animikiins was too busy eating to do more than nod his agreement.

"Yes, he would make someone a good wife," said Gichi Noodin.

Quill froze. So did the other men. The twins even stopped eating, hoping that Quill would spring up and fight. Gichi Noodin shook his hair over his shoulder and raised one eyebrow, looking around as usual to see who was admiring him. But everyone was looking at Quill. Gichi Noodin met Quill's deadly gaze and waved a bone at him as if to say he didn't mean it. Suddenly, Quill laughed. He laughed so hard he began to sputter. He couldn't stop laughing.

Daintily, Gichi Noodin wiped his fingers and puffed out the sleeves of his shirt. He was wearing beautiful beaded garters to keep his sleeves rolled up. Concerned about his hair, he kept flipping it so that it flowed down his back.

"What is so funny?" Gichi Noodin finally asked, seeing that Quill's infectious laugh made others smile.

"Gichi Noodin! You would make a good wife too," said Quill, amiably. "You tend your looks enough for two people. Watch out so girls marry you for love, not just to get your pretty clothes."

Gichi Noodin smiled, because everyone was laughing, but it was clear he didn't quite get the joke.

Quill's hair, coarse and springy, tended to stick out all over his head in the morning. He pretended to smooth his hair down and toss it like Gichi Noodin, but he was the absurd opposite, and this made everyone laugh. Quill's greatest weapon in life was to get people laughing—it was how he solved problems, how he made alliances, and how he got even. Grumpily, confused, Gichi Noodin tried to reach for more food, but his hair swung in the grease and everyone laughed even harder when he panicked and wrung out his raven locks—in fact, there would be no end now to the jokes about his vanity and about how women might want him so that they could wear his ornate shirts and jackets.

# SIX

# TRAIL FOOD

Now that the main part of the work was finished—
the buffalo were skinned and taken apart—it was
time for the longer lasting work to begin: cutting meat
into strips, boiling off the fat, watching the meat dry and
guarding it against dogs, pounding it to meat dust, finding berries or, in this season, herbs and rose hips to pound
into the meat, making it into pemmican. All of this tedious
work, which women did constantly and men avoided, the
boys naturally dreaded. As soon as they could escape, they
ran off to play with their calf and practice shooting. Every
child knew how to make a play bow and arrows from
nearly any material at hand—of course some wood was

better than other wood, and the arrows had to be straight and carefully feathered. Real bows for grown-ups were made with greater care and to a certain style. Makoons and Chickadee had decided that they were ready for grown-up bows, so they decided to gather the materials. For helping her, Two Strike had given each of the boys a good strong knife.

"Let's make bows and shoot some enemy warriors," said Chickadee.

He looked admiringly at the knife that Two Strike had given him.

Makoons had taken sinew to dry and now was twisting it into a bowstring. The calf followed Chickadee down to the stream and watched as his new parent searched for the right wood. It took a long time. They had to find a downed tree, young if possible, but seasoned for a year at least. Ash would be good, and white oak better, but that grew in the hills and back in the prairies. If they settled for the wrong wood, the bow might crack or split. So they kept on looking until they found the right ash tree—then Chickadee worked all afternoon with a hatchet Two Strike had lent them. At last he had long rough blocks of wood that he and Makoons could carve down with their knives.

They would imitate their grandfather. He was a lifelong maker of bows, arrows, and his were considered the finest in the family. Chickadee brought the wooden blanks. As they worked, the little calf fell asleep at their feet. Makoons

imagined how it must feel. When its people had disappeared in the great thunder, and the strange new beings
taken their place, all this baby calf could do was squeeze
its eyes shut in fear and pretend it was invisible. Now that
these beings were feeding and petting him, there was no
way the buffalo calf would let them out of sight. He was
probably afraid that the boys would disappear in the same
way if he didn't stick to them as closely as possible.

Only the thinnest cuts of meat had dried by the second day.
Omakayas had a large bag of rose hips, and Yellow Kettle
had brought Nokomis's dried wild bergamot for flavoring.
Now began the tedious, necessary process of rendering the
fleet, brute, astonishing animals into packs of light, nutri-
tious food.

As soon as any meat fully dried, Omakayas put several
strips on a flat piece of wood. She had a stone that she liked
so much that she had carried it with her for many years.
Nokomis had given her this stone. She had brought it from
the beach on Madeline Island, where Omakayas grew up.
It was just the right sort of stone to grind things with, the
perfect size for a two-handed grip on top, tapering to a gentle rounded bottom. Over the years Omakayas had ground
a hill of berries, a mountain of meat. She began to pound
and grind the meat with the stone, crushing the fibers,
changing the texture until it was light brown, fluffy, pow-
dery. The Juneberries, chokecherries, and pembina berries

weren't ripe yet, or she would have ground them into the meat as well. Then hot buffalo fat would be poured over the pemmican to bind it and preserve it. This food could last for months, even a year. They would take it on trips, or if they had extra they would use it for trading. Yellow Kettle had scraped a hide, dried it out, and made rawhide containers by folding and sewing pieces together. Once the pemmican was finished, they filled four containers. It was a good morning's work.

Yellow Kettle sat back to smoke her little pipe and relax. Omakayas poured a cup of the raspberry and bergamot tea she'd made to refresh the two of them. As they regarded the result of the hard work, a shadow suddenly fell over them. It was Gichi Noodin.

"Here," he said, dropping a huge stinking buffalo hide in front of the two women. "Finish this by tomorrow!"

Omakayas laughed and Yellow Kettle made a snorting noise.

"Why do you laugh, mere women?"

The two now started laughing together.

"Do you mock me?" Gichi Noodin stepped back, glowering with sudden anger.

"Oh no," said Omakayas, "we are laughing at all the others in this camp who can't match your good looks."

"Ah," said Gichi Noodin, tossing his head. "Of course. Many people are comically ugly next to me."

"And they are weak, too," said Yellow Kettle, nearly

70

choking, "compared with your strength!"

"Oh yes," said Gichi Noodin eagerly, pleased that these two women agreed with his opinion of himself. "I am so strong that I am almost *too* strong. You know what I mean?"

"Not exactly," said Omakayas, forcing a puzzled look onto her face. "Could you demonstrate your powers for us?"

"Certainly," said Gichi Noodin, rubbing his hands together. "What would you like me to do?"

"Many people say that women are weak," said Omakayas. "If so, it would be nothing for you to take that beautiful buffalo hide on the ground there, and stake it out over there. Then you could probably work the flesh off with this scraper and rub this mixture of brains and liver into the skin until it softens. I'll bet you could do all of that by tomorrow."

"Ha. You make me laugh, mere woman," said Gichi Noodin. "Of course I could do that. But it would be much too easy. There are other feats of strength I could show you right now. For instance, behold this rock! I can lift it with my hands and bring it down again."

"Not really!"

Omakayas and Yellow Kettle pretended excitement when Gichi Noodin lifted the pounding stone that they'd been using all day.

"Yes, it is true," said Gichi Noodin, putting down the

stone. "I could do this lifting and putting down a thousand times."

Omakayas had certainly done this two thousand times this very morning.

"Unbelievable." She grinned. "What else can you do?"

"I can also jump into the air, quite high."

"How high?" asked Yellow Kettle.

"This high?" asked Omakayas, holding her hand up.

"Jumping? It is nothing to me!"

Omakayas reached over and threw a bundle of sticks onto the fire so that it leapt up.

"Can you leap over this fire?"

"With ease," said Gichi Noodin.

"If you leap the fire we will tan your hide for you," said Omakayas. "If you fail, you will demonstrate your strength by tanning your own buffalo hide."

"It is done," said Gichi Noodin. "Only, please do not insult me. Build the fire higher! I am swift as a cougar, springy as the deer, light as the grasshopper . . ."

". . . dim as the prairie chicken," whispered Yellow Kettle.

". . . and fearless as the buffalo," said Gichi Noodin with great satisfaction. He hardly noticed the amount of wood that Omakayas put on the fire. He was looking around to see who was watching. Ah, he spotted Zozie! She was exactly the one he hoped to impress and there she was, walking toward her mother. Gichi Noodin made some loud groaning noises, as if the noise helped his muscles flex. Then he began fluffing his hair out with his hands so that it would fly out behind him during his great leap.

"Time to prove yourself!" cried Yellow Kettle. "Zozie! Come closer and watch this!"

Gichi Noodin stepped back proudly and rubbed his hands, flicked out his feet. He then began his lunging run toward the fire. As if to greet him, all of the sticks caught fire at once, and the flames spurted high into the air. At the last moment, just as Gichi Noodin launched himself upon his superb jump, he saw that the flames were really, really, very high. His face changed from a look of proud command. His eyes bugged out, his mouth fell open. Upward, he strained. Downward, he fell. Gichi Noodin landed just beyond the flames then tumbled over, yowling. The women clapped their hands to their mouths, trying to stifle laughter. The magnificent fringe on his pants, the soles of his moccasins, and the fancy beadwork apron he wore front and back all had caught fire. He rolled over, hitting at the flames, then sat up. He began to spit on himself to put out the last of the flickering and smoldering bits. Worst of all, the very ends of his long, shining hair had begun to smoke.

"Nooooooo," he cried, batting at his gorgeous tresses.

"Yessss," said Yellow Kettle, lifting the stinky hide. She dropped it at his smoking feet. "Finish this by tomorrow," she said.

# SEVEN

# THE RETURN

On the way back to Pembina, the oxcarts screeched beneath their heavy load of hides. There were parfleches filled with pemmican and huge packs of dried meat. Omakayas had boiled clean a shoulder blade bone for Nokomis to fix to a strong stick and use as a hoe in her garden. Other bones were hollowed out to hold pure fat. Buffalo horns had been kept to hold gunpowder or to make ceremonial spoons. Uncle Quill drove his oxcart with Yellow Kettle and Omakayas riding along. Zozie was riding Whirlwind because Makoons was riding Angeline's horse, Fly. He walked Fly slowly, behind the rest of the trailing camp. She was followed by the lamb and baby buffalo. Both trotted along, trusting and confident, on strong-boned legs. They seemed extremely fond of their mother.

Zozie had grown from an ordinary big sister into a beautiful big sister, but of course her younger twin brothers had not noticed. They did see her shining braids bounce on her straight, graceful back just up ahead of them. They saw how her cloth skirt hugged her legs, how she'd managed to cleverly tie her shawl so that she could carry a large pack of willow wands behind the saddle. She was already a master at making baskets. They knew she had a straight nose, full lips, dark eyes, but the twins were oblivious of the fact that these separate features were put together enchantingly. As a result they did not understand why Gichi Noodin kept galloping his horse just ahead of her. And they really couldn't tell that he was trying to do fancy tricks to impress her. He kept popping up on one side, then the other, of his irritated horse. He kept looking back at her, arching his eyebrows and flipping his hair around. Once, he craned around so far, trying to catch Zozie's eyes, that he ran into Two Strike.

"Do that again and I'll gut you like a fish!" Two Strike growled.

Gichi Noodin just pirouetted away on his furious horse, but stayed carefully out of Two Strike's reach. His saddle had a saddle horn, which could be used to tie a rope. It was the first such saddle anyone had seen. The United States was selling much of its surplus of Civil War army goods. This saddle had been waiting for Gichi Noodin at a trader's store—he'd given many buffalo robes for it. Because it offered a more stable ride, he had learned some special tricks. Using a loop of his reins, he could ride at his horse's flank. He could stand on the saddle. He could turn around and around on the saddle while his horse sullenly galloped in a circle. He did a few of these tricks now, in an effort to captivate Zozie.

"Oh, there he goes again," said Yellow Kettle, rolling her eyes.

Omakayas thought he was amusing, but then suddenly he went past amusing.

Gichi Noodin began to twirl in a circle, legs out straight, holding himself upright on his saddle. Unfortunately, in midtwirl the saddle horn caught the bold red sash at his waist. It caught him from behind. Suddenly, Gichi Noodin was stuck riding backwards on his horse!

Although his horse put up with a great deal, this odd sensation on its back was too much! The horse bolted forward. Gichi Noodin grabbed its tail in an attempt to balance. His eyes bulged with shock, his mouth dropped open in a desperate hoot, which only motivated his horse to move faster.

This ridiculous spectacle was the last anyone saw of Gichi Noodin—that is, until everyone arrived back in the settlement. And even then, he kept an unusually low profile, skulking and slinking for almost an entire day before he regained his pride, his chest puffed out, and he began preening boastfully again.

Nokomis greeted her returning family with excitement, hobbling forward on the cane of diamond willow that Deydey had carved for her. She hugged them and touched their faces. Lovingly, she greeted her great-grandsons. Although the lumps of maple sugar she'd kept in her carrying bags were long gone, she still hoarded little treats for them. Today, she had a comb of wild honey, which she gave them to share. She wouldn't tell them where she'd gotten it, no matter how much they pestered her.

In her family's absence, Nokomis had tended the garden with great contentment. She was very pleased at how lush her beans were growing. Her hills of potatoes were spreading darkly. Her squash vines now sported enormous yellow blossoms. The corn plants rustled with lush energy. Bees, hummingbirds, robins, and Chickadee's namesake foraged and decorated the garden. Nokomis had waited a long time for this glory. She weeded diligently, setting snares for hungry rabbits and raiding gophers. Every day she added a new stick to her fence, which she bound tight with nettle rope or sinew. Deydey had set up a little arbor where people could sit, and they often rested there.

"You've earned the right to sit and watch your plants

grow," he said to Nokomis. She was so old now that everyone claimed her as their mother and grandmother.

"Eyeh, gidebwe," said Nokomis. "You speak the truth."

She rested a moment, gave a deeply happy sigh, then picked up her cane and moved into the garden to adjust a stake or pluck a threatening weed.

# CHAPTER EIGHT

# ENEMIES

The twins were trying to hide from work. And when they couldn't hide, they insisted that training their buffalo ponies was crucial, the most important thing in the world. Yet there was so much to do. The buffalo hides still had to be scraped down. Omakayas and Yellow Kettle had staked them up where the best breezes blew to carry away the flies. Opichi watched over the meat racks, using a willow switch for the flies and a stick against the hopeful dogs. Tiny though she was, she took her job very seriously. Makoons and Chickadee wouldn't have minded looking after the meat, especially since they knew they would not be allowed near the pounding and grinding process, which their mother did in a particular, perfect way. Yellow Kettle also was a perfectionist about the texture and flavor of the pemmican she made. So the boys were saved from any involvement because they always made mistakes.

But the hide tanning job was more difficult to evade.

The boys lit out at dawn, sneaking a cold bannock and some dried meat. All morning, they rode their horses at a dummy made of twigs and bark that was supposed to be a buffalo. They had even stolen some bits of hide to stick on it. Riding past the buffalo, they raised their bows and sank their arrows deep in the spot just over the shoulder where the arrow would reach the heart. They had decided to practice this way first, since it was unlikely they'd have the use of a gun at the next hunt. As they hunted their pretend buffalo, their real calf, who couldn't be without them for a moment, cropped grass nearby. To the mare Fly's relief, at

least one of her strange children had grown up. As the boys rested from their labor of killing buffalo, the calf walked over and put his head down near them, nuzzling them, trying to chew on their sleeves.

"Here we are practicing how to destroy his relatives," said Makoons.

"Don't tell him," said Chickadee, scratching the buffalo calf's head. "He might hate us."

"But a man must live," said Makoons.

"You sound like Gichi Noodin." Chickadee laughed. "A man must do what he must do! A man must keep his pants clean! A man must toss his hair! A man must show his chest!"

"A man must ride his horse backwards holding the tail!"

They collapsed with laughter, which made them hungry. Hungry, they imagined how they might slip back home without alerting their mother, who would force them to help tan hides. How they loathed that laborious and stinky process. And it would be impossible to argue their way out. With no pity in her voice their mother would say she'd loathed the job all of her life, too, but had to do it anyway. They had never yet succeeded in complaining their way out of it.

"We have to slip back in, steal the food."

"We will pretend they are the enemy."

"We are raiding the enemy camp!"

"We must stake our horses near to get away swiftly."

"And slink in under cover of the buffalo calf."

This seemed an excellent idea. First, they painted their faces with stripes of white and black clay. This would make them terrifying if they had to confront an enemy. But they believed their plan would work. They would be mystically invisible. The women were used to the buffalo calf roaming here and there around the cabin, sometimes butting heads with the lamb, sometimes trying to get through Nokomis's fence. Several times she had smacked her cane over the calf's head. Diamond willow is one of the hardest woods that exists, so it must have hurt. The point was, if the buffalo calf wandered into camp the women wouldn't even notice, and if it had eight legs instead of four, they might not notice either. The boys would crouch low next to their calf, steering him with a rope harness until they came near enough food to snatch it with their hands.

Next, they scouted the camp. They tethered their horses and crept close, the buffalo calf on a rope behind them.

"Ah, the enemy is doing just as we predicted," said Chickadee, speaking in a tense whisper.

"They are pretending to prepare hides, while their warriors lay in wait to ambush us."

"Yes, that is their plan. They will pretend everything is normal and take us by surprise."

"We will take *them* by surprise," hissed Makoons. "We will raid their food supply. Our spirit buffalo will help us become invisible."

Closer and closer they crept, while the buffalo innocently munched what it could snatch from the grasses that hid them. The boys agreed to be very careful passing near the garden.

"A very dangerous old warrior watches there," said Chickadee, thinking of Nokomis's cane.

"One with sharp eyes who will warn the others," said Makoons.

They would try to avoid another dangerous warrior, their mother. Sometimes they disobeyed grandmother Yellow Kettle because they were used to her scolding. But they never disobeyed their mother, not only because it was so disrespectful but also because of their father. Animikiins was not to be trifled with either.

When the grass could no longer hide them, they slowly rose and stepped behind the red calf. He was just big enough to shield the two of them as they moved along behind the women, who were intently working on the hides, scraping off the flesh with sharpened tools. As they tiptoed along beside the buffalo, they saw the object of their stealth—the food. Near the pounding stone and bowl, at the fire, which was banked up and barely smoking, there was a small pack, the sort of pack a warrior might need on the trail. It was half filled with nice brown pemmican, a feast for two boys. They edged close without alerting suspicion, and when they were near enough Makoons reached out and grabbed the pack.

But how to leave enemy territory?

The little buffalo would not back up, so they had to turn him carefully and put themselves on the other side of the calf. This they did, most skillfully, tiptoeing, slinking, and at all times keeping watch on the backs of the women as they bent to their task. What they didn't know was that the little arbor that overlooked the garden also overlooked their secret warrior raid. The entire time, Nokomis and Deydey had amused themselves by watching in silence, but now that the boys were about to make a clean getaway they couldn't help themselves.

Deydey suddenly gave a shrill war whoop!

Nokomis trilled a triumphant warning!

The calf bolted. Makoons had his hand in the rope and was carried with him. Chickadee was holding the pack, caught red-handed. There was no buffalo calf to shield him from sight. He darted off. As all three fled, Deydey and Nokomis fell back into their little arbor laughing so hard their bellies ached. When Yellow Kettle and Omakayas came over to find out what was so funny, Nokomis told them about the buffalo warriors, painted for battle. Deydey acted out the part, holding his aching sides. It would be long past dusk before the buffalo warriors dared sneak back to camp. Something worse than enemy captures awaited them, and they knew it: they would be teased without mercy.

Uncle Quill was sitting on a stump by the fire, smoking his little pipe.

"I sense their approach," he said to Animikiins. "The buffalo warriors."

Only the return of hunger forced the boys to try to sneak back home. Having come so late, they'd hoped to slip into the cabin and curl up in their blankets. They froze just out of the firelight circle. Their father spoke.

"My brother, it is best that we not turn around. The buffalo warriors are fearsome. We might embarrass ourselves by shrieking."

"Yet," said Quill, "we, too, are warriors. To not confront

our terrifying enemies will shame us."

"Gidebwe," said Animikiins.

With one movement they turned and jumped out at the boys, giving two screeching war cries. *Their* faces were painted into gruesome war masks! The boys' hearts leapt with horror and they scrambled into the cabin, dived under their blankets, and were silent. The calf wandered loose and Uncle Quill caught it.

"You do look awful," he said to Animikiins.

"I'm scared of you, too," replied the boys' father, as they rubbed the soot and ash from their faces.

"Remember how we used to do those funny, childish things?"

"Sneaking into camp, pretending women were our fearsome enemies, yes."

"Now we just paint ourselves up and scare our sons."

The men turned back to the fire, and sat for a while, staring into the glowing coals. A treaty with the Sioux—the Dakota, Lakota, Nakota people—had kept the peace lately. But both men remembered the years when they'd kept constant lookouts. Animikiins remembered his fear, trying to hide it when he was captured once. He'd been released and even adopted by the Dakota. Things were better, things had changed. Their enemies were different now.

Deydey and Yellow Kettle heard the yells of Animikiins and Quill. Nokomis too. As the old do when they have fewer years left, she forsook sleep for life. She rose out of her blankets and came out to sit with her family, who were pondering this matter. It was an interesting and vital question—who the enemies were.

"Our enemies are bad people of any sort, as ever," said Yellow Kettle. "There are good or bad Sioux, good or bad white people, good or bad Michif people. Good or bad is what makes the enemy."

"But the biggest threat is the people who gobble the land. They are coming. They are white people," said Deydey.

"It is the treaty makers," said Quill, "those who do not keep their promises. I hear Little Shell speaking of the Great White Father—our president. He doesn't trust that one. We have seen what happened in Mne Sota. We have seen what happened to the Dakota."

The four were silent. Some of the Dakota, driven to despair by starving, and by watching their children starve, had attacked settlers. The U.S. Army retaliated. The spirit of cruel chaos had been loosed and in the end the women, the children, the men all suffered. The Dakota were forced from their homeland, imprisoned, executed, force-marched into forbidding lands with no way to live and very little to live for. The land and future would now belong to the settlers. For the Dakota, even those most innocent, there would be a future of exile, hunger, and longing for their beautiful land.

The family stared into the fire. Two Strike came over

and sat down and Quill added more wood.

"We have a good life here, a good hunt; our enemies have not touched us. But we know."

"Yes," said Animikiins slowly, "we know it is only time until the white people want this land, too."

"They sweep us before them," said Nokomis, "like a gobbling wind."

"We hasten our own destruction sometimes," said Deydey. "The traders offer their 'milk,' which is that crazy stuff. Alcohol. Ishkodewaaboo. The liquid that burns."

"I have seen men kill the ones they love," said Quill, shaking his head. "There are some who cannot resist it. I, too, have drunk it. But now I stay clear. Too many bad things happen."

"That is our enemy too, that trader's 'milk,'" said Deydey.

"Remember LaPautre? The drunken skwebii who stole everything from us back in Minnesota? The pitiless man! How he made us suffer."

"If I ever run across LaPautre . . ."

"If I ever see LaPautre . . ."

"If LaPautre ever dares show his face . . ."

"You know, the way he was, somebody else probably killed him by now," said Nokomis.

"You are surely right," growled Two Strike. "I only wish it had been me."

# NINE

## TRADING FOR OTTERS

The buffalo calf butted at the sticks that kept him away from juicy-looking plants—how unfair! He was always hungry. He wandered out to his mother and nudged her for milk, but he was able to digest grass now and she gave him a kick. It hurt. But after all, he was a buffalo and buffalo are tough. He playfully charged his mother, but she calmly sidestepped him and he ran headfirst into a tree. The buffalo calf turned in circles, confused. Then he saw his brothers, the two beings that had appeared before him after the big noise and dust. He knew that if he followed them around long enough, some morsel of strange-tasting but delicious food would come his way. So he happily trotted after them through the camp as they made their way to the trading post.

Pembina was rutted heavily by the passage of oxcarts, and smelled of ox dung, outhouses, and a penned pig or two, as well as cooking fires, roasting meat, and burning garbage. The smells drifted around the boys and Makoons wrinkled his nose.

"Brother, this makes me miss the woods."

"We used to move our camp when it got too stinky!"

"You went to the big city, St. Paul, with our uncle. I bet that smelled worse."

"Gidebwe," said Chickadee. "But oh, that candy was good!"

The boys carried rabbit furs, slung in their belts. They hoped to trade for some sweet stuff—they hoped the trader had some peppermint sticks.

When they reached the store, a large log cabin with tiny windows that could be easily bolted shut, there were a few people from the hunt sitting around on stumps, smoking pipes or talking. One of the men lurched around in a strange way, grabbing at the others, laughing in a high-pitched voice. The boys moved away from him, but they forgot about their earnest little friend, the buffalo calf. He hung right at their heels. As soon as the lurching man saw them, he threw his hands up in the air.

"Awee!" he cried. "There's my little calf! I'll roast him up just fine!"

"Gaawiin!" The boys cried out in alarm. The man's odd gait became a stumble and he swiped at them and tried to seize their calf with his big paws like a drunken bear. A drunken bear! That's what he was, drunk. Both of the boys realized this at once and ran around the back of the trader's cabin. Their calf followed so fast the man couldn't catch them.

"Wah," he cried. "Lost 'em. Where'd they go? Zhooniyaa? Zhooniyaa?"

He was asking all of the others for money, no doubt to buy some more of what their grandfather called "the enemy," traders' "milk." Makoons panted hard. He still had trouble with weakness when he got excited.

"Here, my brother, take the pelts," he told Chickadee. "Sneak past that shkwebi man and buy our candies."

Chickadee took the pelts, slipping around the other side of the building. He watched his chance, then swung in the doorway when the shkwebi man had his back turned. It was dark inside, but his eyes adjusted quickly. The piles of cloth, the bins of cracker-bread, the bags of flour, and the traps and guns fixed to the wall made his head spin.

He walked up to the counter, where the trader's assistant was helping a woman choose some cloth. She was a young Michif woman with a merry face and warm brown eyes. Her black braids were tucked up around her head with flashing-white bone combs. She was taking her time making a decision about the next dress she would sew. There were five bolts of calico spread out before her and she kept touching one, then the other, and tapping her mouth with her pretty finger. Luckily, she noticed Chickadee.

"Oh what a nice boy, waiting his turn," she said. "Please take care of him while I decide."

The assistant turned to Chickadee, who held out the rabbit furs. He had learned how to trade from his uncle the time they went to St. Paul. The assistant, who had flaming red hair and golden eyelashes, was so interesting to Chickadee that he could hardly stop looking at him. He was particularly amazed by the fluffy red curls of his beard, which was the same color as the buffalo calf's hair. Chickadee ducked his head. It was rude to stare. After the young man wrote one set of numbers on a sheet of paper, Chickadee took the paper and studied it. His uncle had taught him the numbers in English—how to say them and how to write them. He wrote down a much higher number on the paper and handed it back to the assistant.

The assistant laughed and said to the Michif lady, "Here is a shrewd one!" He wrote another number down on the paper, between the two numbers.

Chickadee took the paper and frowned at it. He shook his head and wrote a number down between the second and third numbers. The assistant grasped the paper and studied it. He wrote down one more number. Chickadee took the paper and wrote down a different number. The numbers were very close now. The assistant looked over at the young woman and winked.

"All right," he said. "You got the best of me."

Chickadee didn't understand the English, but the Michif lady did and she translated it for him. He burst into a proud smile, and the assistant paid him in chits that could be exchanged for goods in the store. Chickadee looked into the case—oh the wonderful objects! Knives, sashes, metal clips and harness bits, combs, pins, and jars filled with colored sweets. He handed a chit with a small number to the assistant and pointed at the red and white sticks. The assistant handed him four sticks. A small silver pin caught his eye—the shape of an otter. It would look so beautiful on his mother's dress—would Makoons approve? Shyly, he gestured at the pin.

"Oh my," said the young woman, "do you have a sweetheart?"

"My horse is my sweetheart," he said in an embarrassed voice. "The pin is for my mother."

The Michif lady's hand flew to her breast. "Ah," she cried out. "What a bon fee!" (good son).

The assistant looked at the pretty young woman, and slowly drew out not one, but two silver otter pins. They were for either side of a collar or the straps of a dress. He pushed them across the counter to Chickadee, who thanked him while the Michif lady clapped her hands and praised the redheaded, now blushing and happy, assistant. Chickadee put everything inside his carrying pouch. On his way out, he checked on the shkwebi man, who was now stretched out in the shadow of the cabin snoring. Chickadee hopped out the door and rounded the corner to find his brother. Excitedly, they looked at the things their rabbit pelts had bought. Each took a stick of peppermint and began to lick it as they slowly walked back home. Halfway there, Makoons turned around and broke off a bit of candy, giving it to their buffalo calf. The calf's big eyes went liquid with joy. He followed them even closer, pressing his head between them, their best friend in the world.

The two put their candy carefully away as they came back to the cabin—they would savor it as long as they could. Chickadee took out the otter pins. His mother was stirring a buffalo stew over the cooking fire. She was alone. Her sons came up to her and Makoons pulled her skirt.

"What do my sons want?" she asked.

"Turn around, nimaamaa," said Makoons.

She turned around, smiling, and saw that each of her sons held out a shiny pin.

"Onizhishinoon," she said softly.

"They're for you," said Chickadee.

"For me?" She dropped her spoon in the pot. After a moment, tears came into her eyes.

"They are very beautiful," she whispered. "I will keep them all my life."

And she did.

# TEN

# DIAMOND WILLOW

That evening, when the family had gathered, the twins gave Zozie and Opichi each a peppermint stick. Happily, the four youngest sat around the fire, each licking the end of the candy stick into a point, then biting off the point with a nibble, then licking carefully again. Animikiins admired the beautiful otter pins that decorated the straps of Omakayas's dress. He pretended to be jealous and said sternly, "Someone else admires you! Point him out, and I'll chase him down!"

"No, ninaabem, these gifts are from your sons here," said Omakayas.

The boys shifted bashfully, scraping their feet, and the

rest of the family laughed.

"We bought them with our rabbit skins," said Chickadee.

"Rabbit skins?" said Quill. "You must have had a hundred to buy these!"

"No," said Makoons, "we just had twenty."

"Twenty!"

"The Michif lady said that Chickadee drove a hard bargain," said Makoons, proud of his brother.

"The Michif lady?" Zozie laughed. "Did she have a cute face? Did the assistant have red hair?"

"Oh yes!" said Chickadee.

"My brother, you did drive a clever bargain! Your timing was perfect. That assistant is in love with Mariette, the woman you saw. He was trying to impress her, I bet."

"She'll throw him away once everybody gets a good deal out of him," said Yellow Kettle. "She's unscrupulous! Those good-looking ones are very hard!"

"Not all good-looking ones," said Quill. "Zozie is very kind. She caught the eye of Gichi Noodin. She saw the fire in his gaze. She hasn't yet doused the flame!"

Omakayas and Two Strike looked at their daughter in alarm.

"Don't worry." Zozie laughed. "His gorgeous clothes and hair don't impress me. I want a man who rides his horse frontways. But I'll tell you Mariette isn't like that, grandma. She might be in love with that red hair man too, you never know!"

"Doubtful, where that piece of work's involved," snorted Yellow Kettle. "But at least those boys got something very nice for their mother. Next time you boys go in, get me a nice hair comb, will you?"

"You need one," said Fishtail, shaking his head.

"Are you saying my hair is messy?"

"Would I ever call the one like my mother a messy head?"

"Of course you would, no-good son! You're saying it now!" Then suddenly, she began to laugh, stroking at her hair. "Perhaps my husband will beat you to the gift I deserve."

Deydey stood and puffed his chest out like Gichi Noodin. "This old man is still good for something," he said. "When I take in my rabbit furs, I will be sure to go with Chickadee. The hard bargainer."

"No, my father! I will get a fancy hair comb for my mother first!" Fishtail and Deydey squinted and pretended to size each other up with their fists raised. Soon they dropped their hands, laughing.

"He's too tough for me," said Fishtail. "We will get the best comb for Yellow Kettle when the buffalo hides are done, plus other things. We'll have plenty of pails and kettles, maybe a gun, calico, wool trade-cloth, blankets, and ribbons for us all. Even Deydey can tie up his hair in a bow!"

Deydey laughed at that, flipping his hair from side to side like Gichi Noodin.

"Does that please you?" he said in a low voice to Yellow Kettle. The rest of the family expected her to bat him away, but instead she made them laugh even harder by saying yes!

Just after sunrise the next morning, when the world was very still, the buffalo calf rose sleepily and tottered in a circle. The vague memory of the peppermint stick still haunted him, and he was hungry. He remembered that a perfect breakfast could be had in that place surrounded by sticks, which contained the most luscious leaves and goodies for miles around. The cabin and the tents around it were quiet, so he tiptoed, if a calf can tiptoe, up to the edge of Nokomis's garden. He had no idea that the promise in those plants contained the family's winter stores. He couldn't know how much hope and love went into the making of this garden by an old woman who had longed to plant seeds for many years. All he knew was he had four empty rooms in his stomach, each chamber pinching to be filled. When he got to the fence he tried to reach over, but his neck wasn't that long. He put his head down and butted the fence. The wood didn't give. He stepped back, took a little run, and butted again. This time the wood creaked. Next time he'd get through! Again he stepped back and took a run at the fence, but something came down on his head, something hard! The calf stood still, dizzy. A great force surrounded his breakfast! He didn't know what it was. He only knew what he felt. He staggered off to munch tough grass.

Nokomis watched him go. She got up every morning before sunrise to sit in her little arbor and watch her garden wake up to the day. She leaned on her diamond willow cane—already it had come in handy.

# ELEVEN

# THE SORROW OF THE BUFFALO

After that first hunt, the buffalo herds didn't come near again. Time after time, the scouts went out looking. Fishtail, Animikiins, and others from Little Shell's band traversed the distances. They hunted deer, geese, and antelope and brought these home to their families, along with stories of new lands, but they did not find the buffalo. The Strawberry Moon, Ode'imini-giizis passed. Then Aabitaaniibino-giizis, Halfway Moon, was nearly past too.

The little calf was getting big and ranging farther from the boys now, though he always returned. The twins worried that someone would hunt him, but instead, one of Little Shell's best men, whose name was Shield, came to visit one evening. The young buffalo always slept near the cabin, and was standing in its place with the horses when this man arrived with his sacred pipe.

"Can I speak with your buffalo child?" Shield asked the twins.

They agreed, mystified, to be polite. But they thought that Shield might be crazy. They came along with him.

Shield lighted his pipe and smoked it near the buffalo. He offered the buffalo a smoke, which was a sign of great respect. The buffalo calf snorted and tossed its head— which meant either the smoke was bothering his eyes, or he was honored.

"What does it mean when he shakes his head so?" asked Shield.

"It means he is honored," said Makoons.

Shield nodded, ahaw, and spoke directly to the buffalo.

"We have a request. I am asking you to call your people. We miss them. We need them. We will not harm you," said Shield. "But our people need to live. Please help us. Bring us the generous ones."

Shield took some yellow paint from a horn he carried, and decorated the buffalo's forehead. He gave the paint to the twins.

"Put this on him every day," said Shield, "so that the hunters know he is sacred. We have asked him to help us, and I think he will."

***

A few days later, the scouts returned, troubled. They had seen only one small herd of ten buffalo, and at such a great distance that they'd lost them among the gulches of the strange and beautiful carved-up land farther west. One old man said that the buffalo had come from a hole in the earth and could return to live underground at any time they chose. Others maintained that the great herds had stopped traveling up and down the Red River because of something they didn't like.

This thing the buffalo did not like appeared. It terrified and mystified Makoons and Chickadee the very next day, as they were pulling in a big catfish.

They heard a regular pounding noise coming from the south, a great distance away. It sounded like a giant woman was making pemmican with her grinding stone. Their buffalo calf took off like a flash, running back toward the safety of home. Makoons and Chickadee hid on a small overlook, curious but also dizzy with fear. The noise came closer, closer, and then like a mad beast it gave a shriek! The boys tried to run, but their legs gave out. They huddled in the grass and peered at the water. Now it was upon them, and then slowly, grandly, passing them. It was a boat like none they'd ever seen before. Belching blasts of stinking clouds, paddles lashed together into a giant wheel, it screamed again. Upon the huge boat sat a house with people sitting in the windows. Bright flags flew from the sides. Men ran up and down the decks and the boys even saw a woman, clad in an enormous skirt, holding over her head some cloth tied to a pole. Their fear vanished, for obviously the thing did not harm people. Still, they stayed hidden. Makoons and Chickadee looked at each other in wonder.

"Did you see anything like this in St. Paul?"

"Not this," said Chickadee. "There were giant houses, and I heard there were giant boats, but I didn't see one."

Slowly, shrieking, pounding, moaning, it passed them.

"The buffalo don't like this thing," said Makoons.

"Where's our calf?"

"He ran away of course."

"I guess that proves what the people say."

The boat was gone, just noise and disruption and slow swirling water now.

Makoons and Chickadee walked home with the fish they'd caught, and they didn't say much to each other as they walked along. The steamboat was exciting, but also disturbing—if it drove away the buffalo, how would they live?

Finally, the scouts, Fishtail among them, rode into camp with the news of a vast herd, and the little settlement exploded. The carts were loaded, the horses and ponies packed up, the hunters ready. Again, there would be some left behind to keep an eye on the cabins—Deydey, Nokomis, and Yellow Kettle too. This time the Michif people also came along. They brought their priest. He rode

a shambling gray horse and led a pony packed high with all his gear. As the great squeaking, laughing, crying, thundering, living train of people and animals began its journey to the hunt, Makoons and Chickadee took leave of their beloved grandparents. They tried to leave their buffalo calf behind, too, but he insisted on trailing them, grazing as he went. Ever since Shield had given them the paint, they had blazed a yellow mark on his brow and also, for good measure, on his flanks.

"I am worried he'll be sad when he sees his people hunted down," said Makoons.

"Me too," said Chickadee. "I plan to tie some kind of cloth over his eyes."

"Good idea!"

Looking ahead, they saw Gichi Noodin, prancing along as usual with his red and blue finger-woven sash flowing in the breeze, stirred by the antics he put his horse through.

"That sash would make the perfect blindfold."

"It would befit our noble little buffalo brother."

"We can't steal, it would shame our father."

"Though it would not shame Two Strike!"

"Geget! She would be proud of us!"

"Maybe we can trade with him, convince him to give it to us."

The days of travel were long. The boys had plenty of time to devise a plan.

Each evening when the camp stopped, the boys now hunted hard, using the bows that Deydey had perfected. They hunted along the streams and sloughs. Since the winter when they'd had trouble bringing down a partridge from a tree, and Zozie had saved their pride, they'd become so adept with their bows and sharp arrows that they hardly ever missed their game. With the hunters riding ahead to locate the buffalo, the food they killed was important for the rest of the camp. They brought in geese, ducks, muskrats, beaver, rabbits, grouse, prairie chickens, and even gophers. They skinned them all and kept the skins to sell to the trader. Their hopes that Mariette could influence their prices were even better. She was along on the hunt with her family and had left her lovesick trader behind, but they saw Zozie talking with her and nodded sagely at each other. They would make sure the girls were along when it came time to trade.

Omakayas depended on what her sons brought in for her evening stews. There was trail food, pemmican, but they had to make that last as long as possible. Besides, pemmican could be traded for other things they needed. As the boys fantasized that they were mighty, grown-up invincible warriors and lived in their own world of their own making once the camp stopped moving, Omakayas, Zozie, and Angeline worked ceaselessly. They put the camp up, they took the camp down. They dug roots, picked berries, plucked geese and ducks, stitched clothing, worked on hides and governed the children.

In their precious spare time, the women beaded. They beautified cradle boards, bandolier bags, moccasins, fancy leather jackets, pants, and of course dresses for themselves, caps for children. Even blankets got special treatment. Angeline loved making dolls, and Opichi had an entire family of them. She even made a small cloth dog that went everywhere with the doll family. Omakayas had a special design that she loved—it featured her favorite food, the blueberry. She put maple leaves in her design to commemorate the maple trees her family had tapped in the forests of Minnesota. Sometimes she added the outline of a wildflower that captivated her, or the leaves of a plant that presented an irresistible symmetry.

When the buffalo were killed, the camp work would be intensified. Everyone would labor at such a pitch that the women would have no time to talk and bead, so they enjoyed being on the trail.

Even Two Strike left the men and joined the women occasionally, whittling knife handles or repairing arrows. Though she had a gun, she also used her bow. Her lamb had grown into a young sheep, and with its shorter legs had trouble keeping up when Two Strike galloped her horse. For a while it would call after Two Strike, baa, baa, the strange cry of the maanishtaanish. Then it would give up and join the slow-moving camp horses and stay close to its mother, Fly, who had grown to love her lamb and was always happy to have it near her even as it grew and grew.

The light lasted and glowed on the endless grasses of the plains. In the wind, the grasses waved in a mesmerizing flow. The twins didn't notice because they were painting their buffalo for the next day. But Omakayas, who often missed the lakes and trees where she'd passed her child-hood, began to find a special beauty in the waves of grass. She missed the old birchbark houses she'd grown up in, but loved the peace of the tipi. She and Angeline had used tough sinew to stitch together the well-smoked hides. She began to love this new life, and to wonder how she'd lived without the constant presence, the vast mystery of ever-changing sky.

Yet, as they drove on into the great plains, the buffalo seemed to vanish before them. The days were droningly hot, then cooled so fast it felt good to cuddle down in blankets. Manoominike-giizis was upon them, the moon when in their old home they'd picked canoes full of wild rice, their winter food. Still, no buffalo. Now they were becoming scared—the fear could be seen on the grim faces of the hunters. They needed this hunt desperately. Their survival would depend upon it. At night the hunters smoked their sacred pipes and spoke in low tones to the Gizhe Manidoo. The Michif people prayed with their priest. The boys listened to the sounds that their buffalo made, and imitated them. They had decided to learn to speak buffalo, so that they could tell their little brother which way to run. He was now bigger than the two of them put together, and becoming rough, so they begged more paint from Shield, because they were increasingly worried he'd be shot.

Shield was a tall, intelligent, ugly man. His big nose and drooping lips had once made him despair of finding a sweetheart. But he had married a jolly, good-natured woman who gave him two daughters and two sons. He liked children, and when he brought over the yellow paint he stayed to watch Makoons and Chickadee. As they painted their huge little brother, they spoke to him in his language. The sounds were odd and came from deep within the boys' bodies. They also had begun to move in ways that the buffalo understood. They plucked at his new hump and scratched the way a buffalo bird would. They always stood beside him so he wouldn't have to swing his massive head to see them. The buffalo had his ways; they had their ways. But the three of them knew how to get along.

Shield went back to his camp and sat long, smoking his pipe, thinking of what he had just witnessed. Late that night, he went to speak to Animikiins.

# CHAPTER TWELVE

# CALLING BUFFALO

The next morning, as they ate leftover stew from the night before, Animikiins sat his sons down for a talk.

"Shield has told me you are learning your buffalo's ways, even how to speak with him. Is this true?"

The boys nodded with their mouths full. What was so special?

"Shield thinks that what you have learned could help us, help the hunters."

Help the men who the boys idolized? They gulped the stew down.

"How? We can? You want us to help? How? Really?"

The twins spoke over each other, they were so pleased and excited.

Makoons and Chickadee mounted their horses. As always, their buffalo calmly traveled along with them. Together, they followed the hunters. They knew that if they sighted buffalo, there would be a strategy meeting so that the hunters could approach the herd quietly and bring down as many animals as possible. They would have time to make certain that their buffalo was safe, but they hadn't yet acquired Gichi Noodin's sash to blindfold him. As they traveled along, an inspiration came to Makoons. He rode up close to Gichi Noodin.

"What do you want, little insect?" said Gichi Noodin to Makoons. "Be sure you don't get in the way of my powerful hooves."

"Your hooves are indeed powerful," said Makoons.

Gichi Noodin looked at him suspiciously. But Makoons was ready.

"My sister says you are a great warrior," said Makoons.

"She does?" Now Gichi Noodin was much more polite. He slowed his horse so that they could ride along and talk.

"A magnificent hunter, too. And a most unusual man who can do tricks on his horse that put the ordinary man to shame."

"I must admit," said Gichi Noodin, "that she is perfectly

right. I am amazing in so many ways ordinary men are not."

Gichi Noodin stroked his hair as they rode along, and sat higher in the saddle. He had been teased without mercy since his last so-called trick on his horse. So these words were a soothing oil to his spirit. He wanted to hear more.

"Other remarks? Does she speak of me often?" he asked in a hopeful voice.

"She speaks of you so often that nimaamaa has asked her to try and think of something else besides Gichi Noodin!"

"Oho! It's hard for *me* to think of anything else," said Gichi Noodin, "so imagine how difficult it must be for her!"

"Yes, she does go on and on . . ."

"Tell me more—"

"She speaks of the shock she experienced when she first saw your face."

"It probably thrilled her to the core," said Gichi Noodin tenderly.

Now Chickadee had ridden up with the two, and he added his observation. "She couldn't breathe!" He didn't say that Zozie had been laughing so hard that she started choking. He knew Makoons was getting Gichi Noodin softened up to make his pitch.

"Poor woman, back there with the others," mused Gichi Noodin. "She is probably thinking about me this very minute. I wonder what her thoughts might be."

"I can probably tell you," said Makoons.

"Please do," said Gichi Noodin.

"She had a wish," said Makoons slowly. "But it is probably too much."

"A wish? Haha. How could she wish for anything but me?"

"That is exactly it," said Makoons.

"Well," said Gichi Noodin pridefully. "Here I am in all my resplendent glory."

"Yes, exactly," said Makoons again. "But to show that you return her affection, my sister wished that she might have a sign, perhaps your red sash, which she would wear as a sign of her adoration!"

"But my red sash is extremely special," said Gichi Noodin. "It is not only gorgeous, made by my own aunt's weaving fingers, so it cannot be duplicated, but there is another thing. . . ."

"What is that?" asked Chickadee.

"It holds up these pants of the latest fashion, which I bought from the trader on a day when he was looking the other way."

"Looking the other way? You mean you stole it?"

Shocked, the boys glanced at each other.

"Gichi Noodin? Steal? Never. I just borrowed it secretly, until this hunt is over and I can pay him back, of course."

"Of course," said Makoons. "But think of it, Gichi Noodin. That sash could win you the heart of our sister.

And as you are riding on your horse, your pants won't fall off unless *you* fall off."

"Funny boy, that is highly unlikely! In fact, impossible. Gichi Noodin does not fall off his horse!"

"When you dismount gracefully, then," said Makoons.

"Yes," said Chickadee in a respectful voice. "When you leap bravely off your horse, after the hunt we hope, you can reach down with one hand and hold your pants up until you find a different sash."

"True," said Gichi Noodin. "I have another sash, of course, in my tipi. It is not quite as spectacular. But it will do the job."

"Then you could give us the sash now," said Makoons. "Just in case things get confusing. Then we will have this sure mark of your favor, to give our sister this evening."

Gichi Noodin frowned, pursed his lips, and gazed into the distance. Finally, he untied his sash as they rode along and flung it, with a magnificent gesture, to Makoons. As he galloped ahead of them, the twins looked at each other and grinned.

Not long after Makoons obtained the sash from Gichi Noodin, Shield called the boys and their buffalo to the front of the group. They had come to a ridge that overlooked a great expanse of grass. Here, they stopped.

Animikiins and Shield took the boys aside, and gave them a pinch of tobacco. "Do you know what the buffalo sounds like when he wants you to come to him?"

The boys knew that he usually made a long drawn-out sound somewhere between a groan, a grunt, a moan, and a belch.

"Can you make that sound?

The twins made the sound and sure enough their overgrown calf came straight to them.

"Very good," said Shield. "Now will you please stand on this ridge and make that sound over and over to call the buffalo?"

From that moment, until the sun was low in the sky, the twins made the buffalo call over and over. Their calf curled up beside them, for the sound was very pleasant to him. They were hoarse and tired by the time their father told them it was enough. There were no buffalo in sight, and the camp had caught up with the hunters. Tipis were pitched and oxcarts made into shelters. The night had come, the hunt was off, and after eating and talking everyone lay down to rest.

The next morning just after sunrise Animikiins shook his boys awake with excited whispers.

"They came! They came! Get your ponies. You'll ride behind us in the hunt!"

He and Shield were the first scouts of morning and across the vast grass of the prairie they had seen a large herd of thousands. It could be glimpsed now as a dark wavering line across the horizon. Animikiins held his boys to him, and told them that they had done a good thing. He was proud of them. Their grandparents, and their ancestors in the spirit world would also be proud of them. Many of the hunting camp would tell and retell how the twins had called the buffalo. Makoons and Chickadee had helped the people.

When the hunt began, Gichi Noodin nearly spoiled it again by lunging forward and shooting before the party had come close enough to the herd. But the speedy hunting ponies were so eager to run that they quickly closed the gap. Makoons and Chickadee fastened the red sash around their buffalo's eyes and tied him to a tree. Then they mounted their ponies and followed the hunters into the roil of massed buffalo. But their own little buffalo seemed to sense his kindred. He threw his head up. He broke free and with a bleating snort he followed his people blindly. The boys saw him at the same time, running fast as he could. Their buffalo, whom they'd loved and raised, was loose among the others. The red sash might save him from the hunters, but it was tied over his eyes! He couldn't see where he was going at all.

The herd was a rushing thunderous roar. Makoons's and Chickadee's ponies copied the older horses. They rode at breathless speed, trying to catch their buffalo friend. In the chaos, the blindfolded buffalo was seen again and again, bounding with great agility among the others. The boys rode close behind, managed to nearly snag him once, but the power of the moving herd swept them off.

Another amazing sight was seen. It was Gichi Noodin again. In his zeal to be first and kill the largest number of beasts, he steered his horse too close to a great bull, who turned around and charged. The bull knocked into Gichi Noodin's poor horse. It hit so hard that the horse was flung in the air. The horse landed on the ground. So did a pair of new pants. But the owner of the pants, Gichi Noodin, was still going up, up, up, without those pants. He landed on the back of the great buffalo bull, who started in shock, and then went crazy bucking and twirling to release himself from this hateful presence. Somehow Gichi Noodin held on, his bare buttocks flying up and down. It was life or death. His horse had run free. If Gichi Noodin fell, he would be trampled by the buffalo. Panicked, he didn't even realize he'd lost his pants. But then the herd began to slow. Gichi Noodin was able to slide off the bull. He did not know whether he was luckier to have survived the hunt, or luckier to have worn a very long shirt. Unfortunately, his horse was still running, ever more distant, so Gichi Noodin passed among the weirdly quieted animals, raced his way back to camp and dived into his tipi. On the way there, everyone saw him. They would have laughed until they wept, were it not for what happened next.

The strangeness of the animals' behavior stopped the

hunters. The animals walked, even turned toward the hunters, as if allowing themselves to be killed. The hunters cradled their guns and stayed their bows. They walked their horses among the milling beasts, who would not leave their dead brother and sisters. An ominous quiet descended. All of a sudden, the buffalo began to paw madly at the earth.

The buffalo snorted in rage—that was bearable. They gouged at the earth and plowed it with their horns—that was also bearable. But then the buffalo began a slow moaning sound, a low anguished huffing that rose to a wail of pain. Unbearable! The noise swelled and became a vast reverberating cry that raised the hairs on the necks of all the hunters. Now the people in the camp heard it and ran forward, terrified. Makoons and Chickadee cried out. Tears sprang into their eyes, and into the eyes of the older people, for they knew what it was.

"The buffalo people are taking leave of the earth," cried Animikiins, who stood transfixed, beside his sons. "Soon the generous ones will be gone forever."

It took a long time for the herd to disperse, away from the dead they stood near, disconsolate and disoriented. The buffalo walked off, together or alone, a few here or there, until only one buffalo was left. He wore a red sash over his eyes and stood among the dead with his head bowed. Makoons and Chickadee walked up to him, gingerly, fearfully. Before they removed the red sash they turned him so that he would look forward, after his retreating people, not upon so many carcasses. When the sash was pulled off he stared into the distance, as in a trance. Makoons had tears in his eyes. Chickadee petted his friend, trying to console him. But their buffalo didn't acknowledge the brothers or respond to them in any way. He had seen the truth of things. This was how things really were. So he just began to walk. Leaving the dead behind him, and the humans who lived off his people's flesh, he went to be with his own.

That night the feasting was subdued—that is, until Gichi Noodin was dragged from his tipi into the camp. Then it got ugly. The hunters had been talking, and Little Shell and Shield had decided. Gichi Noodin had once again nearly stampeded a herd, nearly cost them the hunt, because of his greedy ways. He would not be allowed a third time. Two men brought him into the circle, near the fire. Another two men left his aunt and her family weeping, but perhaps secretly relieved, and brought all that Gichi Noodin owned. His gun was taken from him and given to a man with a very large family to feed. His bow was given to Two Strike, who broke it between her thighs and threw the halves down at Gichi Noodin's feet. He gulped. His clothing was divided up. His shield was burned. His hair was in a long braid. A woman sawed off the braid with a knife. Gichi Noodin took the braid in his hands and stared at it, in shock. He was wearing a pair of leggings, a breechclout, and his second-best sash. A woman removed his sash. He had to beg to keep his shirt and one old blanket. Contemptuously, Two Strike kicked her knife to his feet. He had violated one of the tribe's strictest laws. A law that could mean starvation, were it not followed. Everybody turned their backs on Gichi Noodin. Everyone except Makoons.

Gichi Noodin slowly bent over and picked up the knife. His hair stuck out in a bush. He seemed small, suddenly, and lonely and plain. As he stood up, Gichi Noodin saw Makoons, who held out the fine red sash.

Makoons gave the sash to Gichi Noodin, who saw in it the failure of his charm, and Zozie's rejection. But also, well, it was a beautiful sash! Makoons could see that the sash cheered Gichi Noodin slightly. At least he had something attractive to wear as he was banished to wander alone.

# THIRTEEN

# THE PATH OF SOULS

During the butchering this time, the flies were terrible. They came down in sheets and bit viciously. They covered the drying meat. They covered the carcasses, laying their eggs, crawling in black waves over everything. The women lighted smudge fires to drive them off, and smoke the meat. Omakayas, Angeline, and Zozie tied pieces of cloth on their heads because they hated the feeling of flies crawling through their hair. The sun superheated the earth, and more flies, of every sort, hatched and arrived to torment the camp. The butchering had to be done swiftly, and everyone worked through the nights. Still, some of the dead buffalo had to be abandoned to the vultures, the ravens, the crows, and the wolves. This waste went against everything that Animikiins believed, and he regretted killing so many. At night, stained with blood, covered with biting flies, he prayed for forgiveness. Beside him, Omakayas also spoke to the Gizhe Manidoo, and Makoons and Chickadee, Opichi and Angeline, Fishtail and Uncle Quill listened. They were too exhausted to speak, so they just bowed their heads.

At last the hunting party, with as much meat and as many skins and robes as they could dry or save, made their way back to Pembina. The wind rose and swept up the flies in a droning cyclone. The days cooled and the air was crisp in the morning. A tremendous relief lifted people's spirits. The buffalo berries, Juneberries, and chokecherries were ripe. Makoons and Chickadee picked as many berries as they could whenever they stopped to camp. The women took turns driving the oxcart, sometimes riding horses or walking. As they rode along, there was always a skin covered with berries drying in the cart behind them. They would add the dried berries to the pemmican. They'd add dried berries to everything! Although Yellow Kettle always scolded the twins when they ate berries while they picked, she wasn't there, so they disobeyed. Omakayas didn't stop them. The journey was good, but still, they couldn't wait to get home. They wanted to see how Nokomis's garden had fared, to rest a little, to be all together again.

"Let's ride ahead!" Makoons called, pressing Whirlwind into a gallop.

Chickadee was riding Sweetheart. Both horses pricked up their ears and the boys raced for the cabin, where Nokomis and Yellow Kettle waited under their shady arbor. Even with her poor hearing, Nokomis knew the sound of the oxcarts. She saw the boys through cloudy eyes and hobbled forward.

Nokomis's garden was full-grown! The boys staked their horses in the grass and walked through the gate of sticks. There was corn, nearly ripe. A sunny little field of it. The spotted beans bulged in their  green cases. Squash vines with giant leaves twined across the earth. Here and there a green squash ripened to gold. There were hills of potatoes with spiky leaves blanketing hidden treasure. So much food!

"When will the corn get ripe?" asked Makoons, his mouth watering.

"Soon," said Nokomis. "You boys must help me guard it. I'm getting tired of sitting here with my stick handy!"

They had to tell her what happened to their buffalo,

and she said that she was sad to hear it, even though he had wanted to eat her garden. Deydey sat down and asked them to tell everything.

"Lots of things happened," said Makoons.

He and Chickadee told about Gichi Noodin and then, in a halting way, for it hurt to even remember, they told how the buffalo had behaved after the hunt. They told of the buffalo's wild and lamenting sounds, a crying that had chilled their hearts. Nokomis was quiet—she understood.

Omakayas and Nokomis picked the corn, talking of the old days when they had guarded the fields on Madeline Islands from the crows and blackbirds, and how Omakayas had saved one crow and made it her pet. They braided some of the ears of corn, and hung them to dry. This would be winter food. They ate stews of squash and beans, but dried the beans in the sun, too, and cut the squash into strips and packed it. All of this made Nokomis so happy, each day, that her eyes sometimes watered with the sheer joy of it.

"Just think," she said, "this is my own garden, come to life again, after all the years we have spent wandering."

"Giizhaawenimin, Nokomis," said Omakayas, touching her grandmother's cheek. Grandmother's skin had become extremely soft. She was frail now, but pushed herself to work every day because of the plants. She peppered Omakayas with advice, with knowledge, with teachings about the plants she grew and wild plants, too. Nokomis was proud that she, an old woman, was providing for her family. This gave her rich pleasure. Every morning, she was out at sunrise, sometimes smoking her little pipe, pulling weeds, always smiling. By the time the boys sleepily rose from their blankets and went outside, she had a small cooking fire going and tea, from her bee balm plants and wild mint, would be ready for them to drink. Sometimes she also crushed rose hips, or wild raspberry leaves. Everyone drank her teas to help them stay strong.

One morning, just after sunrise, Omakayas heard her grandmother go out. She closed her eyes and fell back into a light, comforting sleep. Nokomis walked into her garden. Nokomis greeted the sun, her palms out, smiling. Then she lay herself carefully down between the rows of gentle plants—it was comfortable there. As Nokomis lay on the earth, she felt a lightness in her body. She had no aches, no pain in her body at all. Suddenly, to her surprise, she felt herself rise out of her old body. She looked down at her old body, lying peacefully on the ground.

"At last, my time has come," she said in wonder.

She said good-bye to her sleeping family. Good-bye to this world.

Peacefully, she turned to the west. A path opened before her. She saw someone familiar and laughed. Her old friend Tallow! Nokomis stepped onto the path. She looked down at her cane, dropped it, and began walking lightly away.

\*\*\*

Shortly after Nokomis had departed on her journey, Omakayas woke up. She came out into the garden and found her grandmother. The diamond willow cane lay beside her. She looked as though she was asleep, dreaming, but Omakayas knew that she was not. She took her grandmother's hand and sat on the ground beside her. She thought of all that they had been through together. Nokomis had endured it all, never complaining, never losing her temper, never taking out her anger on her children, grandchildren, or great-grandchildren. Nokomis had taught her with every action how to exist.

"Journey well," Omakayas whispered. "I will try to be like you."

Deydey lighted the ceremony fire, and for the next four days it burned to light the way for Nokomis's spirit along its path. Omakayas cut her long hair and offered it in mourning. Chickadee cut his braid off too. Weeping, he threw it into the fire. Makoons fingered his hair but during his illness it had become so thin and crackly that it wasn't a very good offering. Still, he sliced his braid off. As he threw it into the fire, he whispered to his grandmother.

"Nokomis, I don't have much. This is all I have to give."

"Journey well," said Deydey. "Your loved ones will watch out for you every step of the way."

Everyone took turns feeding the fire, bringing wood, staring into the flames. As they sat alone, one or the other looking into the flickering light, sometimes her face would appear. Sometimes they saw her walking, her step light, never looking back.

The family took all the seeds from the garden and then they buried Nokomis there, deeply, wrapped in her blanket with gifts and tobacco for the spirit world. They buried her simply. There was no stone, no grave house, nothing to mark where she lay except the exuberant and drying growth of her garden.

Nokomis had said:

"I do not need a marker of my passage, for my creator knows where I am. I do not want anyone to cry. I lived a good life, my hair turned to snow, I saw my great-grandchildren, I grew my garden. That is all."

FOURTEEN

# THE PATH OF LIFE

I t was hard to admit. The people were reluctant to understand. But it was true—the buffalo were moving west.
The great herds would avoid the settlements, the river with
its screaming steamboats. After Nokomis was buried, the
family decided to stay with Little Shell's people and talked
of leaving Pembina. But Angeline and Fishtail wanted to
stay in the cabin with Opichi. When Makoons heard this,
it troubled him. He did not know why.

Several times Makoons spoke with Fishtail, begging
him to come along, to bring his family. Fishtail smiled at
his nephew and reassured him that they would be together
next summer, when the buffalo came. But they would

winter here, in the cabin. Makoons didn't know why this was so important to him. But every time Angeline stoked his hair, reassuring him in her own way, saying that they would travel, they would see them soon, they would surely bring Opichi, Makoons turned away with tears in his eyes. He didn't know why.

They had made friends among the Michifs, Fishtail explained. The family of Antoinette, a friend of Quill's, was going to trade their hides in St. Paul. They might join them! Fishtail had followed Quill's instructions and made an oxcart. As a young girl, Angeline had learned to read and write in a school back on Madeline Island. She wanted Opichi to learn as well. There was a small school in Pembina.

"Please, please come anyway," begged Makoons.

He didn't know why.

The rest of the family, along with Little Shell's people, decided to travel to a place farther west. It was an area of low hills, surrounded by the plains. These hills were rich with oak and birch trees, with every sort of game. There was shelter from the wind during the long harsh winters of the great plains. This had long been a coveted stopping place, a center for trade, with lakes to fish and nuts and berries to gather.

This place was called the Turtle Mountains.

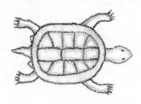

The nights were getting cold as the family started out. With Deydey's knowledge to guide them, they would build a log cabin there before the snow fell. As they crossed the plains, they came to a deep but gradual ravine and an old riverbed. From it rose the highest hill they had ever seen— they had heard of mountains, farther west, that parted the clouds. Those mountains were rumored to be covered with snow. They climbed this hill to see how far they could see— they stayed there looking into the distance, at what would be their new home in the west. Makoons still had a troubled feeling every time he looked east, back toward Pembina. He told his brother about this feeling and Chickadee was silent, for he remembered his brother's dream.

On and on they forged their way, passing among sloughs rich with migrating ducks, geese, and every sort of wild bird. There was frost in the grass now, in the mornings, and even the afternoon sun held only a hint of warmth. They hurried. Then one day as the ox plodded and the cart rocked and shrieked, as the horses walked, laden, as the dogs slunk along behind, Omakayas had a feeling. She sensed something before them—trees. They scented the air. The fragrance of leaves and forest earth reminded her of all she'd left behind well before she saw the green oasis on the plains. It reminded her of home.

The family found a good piece of earth with water and dense groves of oak, birch, poplar. They cleared brush and

cut down the straightest birch and popple trees, skinned off the bark and leaves. Two Strike, Animikiins, and Quill notched the ends with hatchets and fitted them together, and Omakayas, Yellow Kettle, and Zozie followed with gobs of clay dug out of the water and beside the stream. They mixed the mud with dried reeds and grass, and pressed the mixture between the logs. When the mud dried it would form a seal to block out the wind.

In the woods, from great fallen trees, they lifted sheets of bark for the roof. To the roof's framework of poles, they tied the bark with sinew and strips of buffalo hide. Beneath the bark, on the inside, they fixed more rawhide, wetted it, and even stretched it to fit over a frame to make a door. The family agreed that the cabin was very snug. It even had a small stove, a small iron box with legs that Quill had bought with his last robes. He'd bought a stovepipe, too. Animikiins cut a hole in the wall for it. The cabin was complete. Two Strike pitched the plains tipi beside the cabin and said she'd sleep there, cuddled up with two dogs and her lamb, which was now full-grown. The family began work on a lean-to shelter for the horses. When that was done, they cut and gathered as much grass as possible. Zozie was the one who tied the grass up in a tree—it was emergency food for the horses. Within a week, the snows began, lightly, melting away once, then clinging to the hard frozen stems of grass.

Inside the cabin, Omakayas and Yellow Kettle hung blankets on the wall, lined the sleeping areas with buffalo robes, skin side on the stomped dirt floor. Two Strike did the same in the tipi, which she preferred. She built a fire pit in the middle, and gathered great heaps of wood. Makoons and Chickadee were kept busy. They dragged dry branches from the woods. They cut them into pieces, taking turns with Two Strike's hatchet. Omakayas kept a space clear around the stove, and from the rafters set straight across the roof she and Zozie hung rawhide sacks of pemmican, bags of dried squash and beans, braided ears of corn, sacks of berries, salt, dried meat, dried nettles, raspberry leaves, rose hips, and other teas that they could use for medicine.

In one corner of the cabin, Deydey dug a deep hole and filled it with sand from the lake, which lay just through the woods. They buried all the potatoes from Nokomis's garden, the squash, the wild roots, in this sand. The sand would keep the potatoes and all else just the right temperature through the winter. They covered this stash with bark.

By the time this was done, Deydey was using Nokomis's cane. He and Yellow Kettle were growing old, Omakayas realized. And in his kindness, which was so different from Yellow Kettle's unexpected angers, she found solace.

The boys in sleep always curled up near their grandfather. With Nokomis gone, they too relied on the sweetness and wisdom of his age.

The wind howled around them for three days—but it did not bring a blizzard. Only a dusting of snow. They could hear branches cracking to earth, branches thrashing in the woods. They had a rope tied to the lean-to and went out from time to time to check the horses. These horses knew how to survive in any weather. Their coats were thick. They huddled together, but they also had made a path into the trees where they could eat some of the grasses that grew in clearings. The snow was not deep there because the dense trees blocked the raging wind.

Inside the little cabin, they talked and slept. They missed Nokomis very much because of the stories she'd tell during winter times when they were stuck inside their long-ago birchbark house. At first everyone was simply sad, thinking of how she'd start her tales, Mewinzha, mewinzha, a long time ago.

And then suddenly Omakayas said those words.

Mewinzha, mewinzha, Omakayas began.

A young man lived all alone. He didn't know how he

came to be without his family. He didn't know who he was. He was just a young man. Every morning he went out to hunt. He was an excellent hunter, never missed a shot. The one animal he never hunted was the bear, however, because he admired bears and loved them for some reason.

One day, he snared a fine rabbit. When he brought it home to eat, he noticed someone had been in his lodge. A fire was laid. Water boiled in the kettle. Everything was cozy and warm. At the foot of his bed he found a pair of beautiful moccasins. He put them on his feet, admired them, and said, "I hope it was a woman who came here. Tomorrow I'll hunt earlier, and I will meet her."

The next morning, he hunted earlier. This time he killed a rabbit and several partridges. When he came home he again found a cheerful fire blazing, water boiling for soup, and at the foot of his bed another pair of nice moccasins. "I have missed the woman once more," he said, "but I will hunt even earlier tomorrow. Surely I can catch her!"

Now he wanted very much to find this woman, for he was lonely. He was tired of being alone and always talking to himself. He could tell that she was very capable. Everything was so cozy and nice it made his heart ache to find her. So he went out hunting earlier than ever, and this time he killed a large moose. He brought back the choicest parts only. When he came to his lodge and saw the smoke riding from the fire inside he started to run. There she was. He saw her coming from his house.

"Wait, stop," he called.

The woman turned and smiled at him. She was friendly and sweet.

"Do not leave," he said. "I have killed a fine moose. We can make a good soup."

At this, her eyes lighted up.

"A moose! That is very good. My father and his people are so hungry. Their hunting is going badly. Perhaps we can bring the meat."

"With pleasure," said the young man.

He went back with the woman. Together they packed out the moose meat on a toboggan. As they were nearing the man's lodge, he saw another moose and killed it too. They butchered that moose and made a drag from the moose skin. They managed to get all of the meat back to the lodge.

"We will have a tough time bringing this food, and all of my things, to your people," said the man, looking at his possessions and at all of the bundles and pieces of heavy meat and hide.

"Turn around, do not watch me," said the woman.

When the man turned away, she stepped on each bundle. Everything she stepped on disappeared into the ground. The man was greatly surprised when he finally turned back. He wondered what she had done, but decided to accept it. They shouldered the few belongings that remained and set off.

That night, they reached a place to camp.

"What now?" asked the man.

The woman stamped her foot on the ground. The tent came out of the earth just like that and set itself up with blankets on the ground, nice and cozy. She stamped again. The kettle and enough meat for their dinner appeared.

"Let us make ourselves comfortable," the woman said.

So they ate, and slept, and the next day she let the man watch her step on each pack before it disappeared. By the middle of the day, the two reached her father. He rushed from his lodge, poor and ragged. Her family rushed out with them.

"Here he is! Our son-in-law!" they shouted.

The woman stamped her foot over and over. Each time she stamped, meat appeared, and of course their tent and blankets. The entire family feasted together, and the man was wondrously happy. He had fallen in love with the woman and her mystic ways.

"How did you know about me?" he later asked her.

"We are all bears," said the woman. "We watched you in our other shape. We noticed that you never hunted our kind. You surely could have killed a lot of us, for you are a great hunter. We are grateful you left us alone. Will you become a bear and live with us?"

"Gladly," said the man.

And so he did, and they were happy, and lived a long time peacefully in their bear village.

That is all, mi'iw minik.

Makoons woke to the sound of his family stirring about. He realized he'd been listening to the wind in his dreams. The cabin had two windows—they were covered with finely scraped rawhide. During the great wind the light had flickered, but now the windows glowed and he could feel cold penetrating every tiny space and crack between the poles and the tamped-in mud. The air was finally still, and the sun was so bright.

Stepping outdoors, Makoons blinked at the reflection off the shallow new snow. He and Chickadee wore strips of fur wrapped around and around their feet. Rabbit-fur boots with the fur turned inward. They wore two pairs of woolen pants, deerhide shirts, vests of rabbit fur with wool trim.

They had fur hoods and coats made of trading blankets. They wore fur mitts. Two Strike, Quill, and sometimes Animikiins walked around in the cold wearing a blanket or a warm jacket, nothing special—but Omakayas, Zozie, and Yellow Kettle, especially, were determined to keep their family warmly clothed. The women themselves wore two or three skirts, fur vests, heavy shawls, and rabbit-fur caps. They had made their moccasins with tough buffalo hide soles and the curly side of the buffalo robe beneath their feet. Everyone had dressed up because they had decided to take the horses to visit a small trading cabin they had passed. In a week or so, the snow might fall too deep. There would be a blizzard, closing them in. There was also a school in the Turtle Mountains. They hadn't known about this. They wanted to see about it, and wished that Angeline and Fishtail had known. They might have come along.

Two Strike, who had slept in the tipi with her maan-ishtaanish and plenty of wood to keep her fire going, used Nokomis's buffalo-shoulder hoe to heap snow against the tipi for insulation. The horses had kept circling and trampled out a place for themselves—the wind passed over them. But they were hungry. Makoons and Chickadee went out to the woods to get some food for them. They cut thin willow wands and what dry grass had escaped the snow—there were plenty of places where swirling snow left the earth nearly bare. For the ox, they cut away the outer bark of willow and elm, and slashed off the juicy inner bark. They were careful not to cut all the way around the tree, for that would kill it.

The trading store was a tiny cabin, hung deep with furs, but there wasn't much to trade for because no supplies had come in. Still, several people had gathered to talk. They sat around on the floor and looked up when the family entered. Only Omakayas and Yellow Kettle had stayed home. Everyone else stopped and stared, in shock, at the person who stood up slowly to greet them.

It was Gichi Noodin, but greatly changed. His once smooth cheeks were disfigured with deep scars. His once lustrous long hair was dull and ragged. His clothes were thin and torn. He wore no moccasins, only rags and strips of leather around his feet. He still wore his once beautiful red sash, now in tatters. But most different of all was his bright smile of delight when he saw the family, and the look in his eyes. It was hard to describe at first, Zozie told Omakayas later. It was as though his eyes looked *outward* for the first time. Before, he'd seen only his own reflection in his mind, or the eyes of other people. Now, he was truly looking at people. Not thinking only of himself. When he saw Two Strike, he beamed and held out the knife she had given him.

"I am truly grateful to you, Two Strike," said Gichi Noodin. "If it weren't for the knife you gave me, I would never have survived."

"How's that?" Two Strike was shocked at the change in Gichi Noodin. Maybe he'd gone crazy! With an unusually gentle gesture, she laid the knife back in his hand and told him that he must keep it.

"Miigwech," said Gichi Noodin. "This is my only weapon. My only tool. I'm glad to have it!"

"What . . . happened to you?" asked Two Strike.

For the first time ever, Gichi Noodin spoke humbly.

"You know me, I bumbled about and lost my way. I wanted to get here, but wandered around! Then I was walking along a hilly ridge when I felt eyes on me. You know the feeling? There was an itching between my shoulder blades. I took the knife out. I turned around and around in a circle. Then I saw that I was being stalked by a cougar. As I circled, it circled. You must never turn your back on a cougar, of course. The cougar screamed at me. I screamed back. We circled each other for an endless time, then the cougar, who must have been terribly hungry, gathered herself and threw herself upon me. She was huge, and I was sure at first that I would die. But I got lucky, so lucky! With this knife I was able to kill her. Then I was able to skin this cougar, so I had something to keep me warm at night. I ate the cougar too—I usually don't like cat meat, but this time it tasted marvelous to me. I wandered some more, starved some more. Had many interesting dreams! I didn't have any visions, though! I guess those are for greater men. I kept the cougar's claws and made these"—he removed two necklaces from a pouch. From painstakingly woven strands of cat sinew dangled the claws of a very large cougar. One, he gave to Two Strike. The other, he gave to Zozie.

Then, of all things, he walked outside and away before they could even thank him, admire him, or give him something in return.

Two Strike put the necklace on with a thoughtful smile. "I wouldn't know him. It's not even the scars—it's the way he is now."

"I know," said Zozie. "And his face was *too* perfect before, you know? It was sort of scary. Now, to my mind at least, Gichi Noodin is much better-looking."

Nobody spoke. Zozie suddenly blushed when she saw their faces.

"Not that I care," she said hastily, but too late.

Soon after the family returned to their cabin, Two Strike also returned to her tipi.

A cry of rage and sorrow split the air.

Makoons and Chickadee ran to her. The two dogs she'd left to guard her sheep had instead killed it. Her fury was horrible to witness. Her teeth gnashed and the dogs groveled on the ground before her. She had no pity. Although these dogs hunted with her and slept near her for warmth, they had betrayed her. With a single quick swipe, she killed the first dog. Her knife flashed. The other was dead. Makoons and Chickadee were somber, and turned away to see that their mother had also seen what happened. There was a strange expression on their mother's face, and as they walked back to the cabin she spoke.

"That exact thing happened when I was a little girl. Only I was the one the dogs threatened. Tallow, the old woman I always loved, killed her mean yellow dog to protect me."

That day, the boys helped Two Strike as she mournfully skinned the hide off her poor pet. She began to clean and work on the hide, but told the boys to give the carcass to their mother.

"I loved this animal. I can't eat it. But it should not go to waste," said Two Strike.

It snowed once. Snowed a little again. Then one day a real blizzard started. Makoons and Chickadee were out setting snares for rabbits. They hurried back. At first the snow was swirly and light, but very quickly it came down in blasts. The wind blew wild. Suddenly the blizzard whitened the air, the snow so fine and thick you had to breathe it in. Makoons and Chickadee made certain of the horses and followed the rope trail to the cabin. They fell in the door. Already the snow had driven itself down their necks and covered their hair. They shook it off and curled in their blankets, near the stove.

Omakayas was stirring up a fragrant stew. Animikiins had killed a deer and they had fresh venison. She added some of the potatoes, squash, and dried pembina berries. The boys ate gratefully, and nodded off. The snow stormed down all night, all the next day, and the next day after that. Animikiins had tied a rope all the way around the cabin to

Two Strike's tipi—she had been so sad when the blizzard began that she wouldn't come into the cabin. She preferred to stay alone. Now they were worried about her.

Animikiins was gone a short while, then he fell back in the door. Two Strike was fine, he said. She was sitting by a roaring fire. Out of her sheepskin, she'd made a soft pillow. The dogs? She'd eaten well, she said, and wasn't hungry. In one corner, there was a neat pile of bones.

The snow would remain deep, impassable, and the family had to snowshoe in and out of their camp. The horses, turned loose in the woods, found forage and returned each night. Manidoo-giizisoons, Little Spirit Moon, and Gichi-manidoo-giizis, the Big Spirit Moon, passed before they had a visitor.

It was a clear cold day. The snow dazzling, the sky a deep blue. Omakayas's dogs, who slept with the horses, ran out to bark a warning. From the doorway, she saw Gichi Noodin make his way through the woods, on snowshoes. On his back there was a bundle. From the bundle a familiar face peeped. Opichi.

Omakayas cried out and ran from the house.

Makoons hid his face. Somehow he had sensed this visitor had to do with the fear he'd had on leaving his aunt and uncle in Pembina. Somehow, back then, he'd known they might never see one another again in this world. When he came to the doorway, trembling, he saw Opichi and knew her parents were gone for good.

Later, in the cabin, with Opichi and her little doll family sleeping exhaustedly in a corner, Gichi Noodin told the story.

When the trading supplies were brought from Pembina to the Turtle Mountains, he said, the driver of the cart told of an illness that had swept away many people early that winter. Just as the people moved indoors, the illness had taken hold. It was a sort of choking sickness. Nobody knew what to call it. The sickness took Angeline. Then it took Fishtail. It nearly took Opichi. The child needed her family.

When Gichi Noodin heard this, he had walked from the Turtle Mountains all the way back to Pembina. Then he turned around and walked all the way back to the Turtle Mountains with Opichi, the Robin, on his back.

"When I was tired, she would sing little songs, to pick up my spirits," said Gichi Noodin. "Mariette made a nice fur sack for Opichi, so she wasn't cold. We ate pemmican and jerky. We even had a few sticks of hard candy, eh? If we were thirsty, we melted the snow. Now Opichi knows how to survive, too. We traveled well."

Omakayas put her face in her hands. For a long while, she could not move. She mourned her sister, and Fishtail, who'd loved them all. She kept seeing her sister's scarred beauty, grown deeper through the years. She kept remembering Fishtail's courage and kindness. Their happiness when Opichi came to brighten their world.

Yellow Kettle fed Gichi Noodin, but nobody else had the heart to eat. They sorrowed as a family. The cabin was full of weeping. But as they didn't want to wake Opichi, they all cried quietly. After a long while, they finally slept. The next morning, when Gichi Noodin made ready to leave, Animikiins gave Omakayas a significant look. She put her hand on his arm.

"Where are you going?"

"Nowhere," said Gichi Noodin, looking down at his feet.

"Then why don't you stay here?"

Animikiins had to admit that during his long moons of survival, Gichi Noodin had become an extremely clever hunter. Deydey had to admit that during his long moons of boredom, Gichi Noodin had become a very funny storyteller. Omakayas said from the beginning that he had saved her sister's child, who was also her child in the Ojibwe tradition, and that in this way he had become family. She loved Opichi very much. Although Opichi missed her parents, she was still very young, and quickly attached herself to Omakayas. Opichi also couldn't help being merry sometimes, making people laugh. Opichi loved Gichi Noodin, of course. Makoons and Chickadee had to admit that he could make a winter fire from scratch faster than they could—it was a skill they'd made into a competition. Yellow Kettle had to admit Gichi Noodin never let the wood run low. Two Strike had to admit he threw a knife about half as well as she could. They played the game of hitting a target across the tipi, a piece of wood. Wood lice woke up in the heat and crawled across the log. Gichi Noodin speared them with the point of his knife. Yes, he was pretty good at that. But although everyone expected he might brag, at least a little, they had to admit that he had become surprisingly modest. And Zozie, well, she had to admit nothing. She didn't have to speak. She said it all with her eyes.

One night Makoons and Chickadee lay awake, side by side in the fading glow of the little stove.

"My brother," said Chickadee, "do you remember when you were ill? You had a dream?"

"Yes," said Makoons.

"Is it over? Was this all? Losing Nokomis? Then our aunt and uncle? Opichi losing her parents? Was this all?"

Makoons said nothing.

"Brother," said Chickadee. "Your dream. Is it over?"

Makoons still said nothing.

"Brother?"

Makoons sighed deeply, pretended to have fallen asleep. But his eyes were open, staring into the darkness.

The End
Mi'iw minik

# AUTHOR'S NOTE
# ON THE OJIBWE LANGUAGE

Obijbwemowin was originally a spoken, not written, language, and for that reason spellings are often idiosyncratic. There are also many, many dialects in use. To make the Obijbwemowin in the text easier to read, I have sometimes used phonetic spellings. I apologize to the reader for any mistakes and refer those who would like to encounter the language in depth to *A Concise Dictionary of Minnesota Ojibwe*, edited by John D. Nichols and Earl Nyholm; to the *Oshkaabewis Native Journal*, edited by Anton Treuer; to the work of Brendan Fairbanks; and to the curriculum developed by Dennis Jones at the University of Minnesota.

# ACKNOWLEDGMENTS

Miigwech:

To Netaa-niimid Amooikwe, Persia, for consultation on Ojibwe language, horse behavior, horse riding, and horse training. To Nicholas Vrooman, whose book *"The Whole Country Was . . . 'One Robe'": Little Shell's America*, is an invaluable source. George Catlin recounted a story of a tame buffalo calf that follows him around camp after a hunt. Thanks to Ron Manson for sharing his knowledge of the fish that inhabited the original waters of North Dakota. Thank you to Dolores Manson for her example as a mother, grandmother, and ceramic artist. Miigwech Denise Lajimodiere for our conversation about buffalo hunts and her memories of her grandfathers' stories. The story of the tremendous sorrow of the herd of buffalo is true. It was told by Gregoire Monette of Langdon, North Dakota, and first printed in the *Courier-Democrat Newspaper* at Langdon in 1917. The story of the man who married into a family of bears is adapted from a story titled "The Bear Woman," told by Coming Day, in the book *Sacred Stories of the Sweet Grass Cree*, edited by Leonard Bloomfield. Most of all, I want to thank my parents, Rita Gourneau Erdrich and Ralph Erdrich, for the stories they tell me, the work they do, and the way they make life new and interesting every single day.

# GLOSSARY AND PRONUNCIATION GUIDE OF OJIBWE TERMS

**aadizookaan** (ahd-zoh-kahn): a traditional story that often helps explain how to live as an Ojibwe

**aadizookaanag** (ahd-zoh-khan-ahg): the plural form of **aadizookaan**

**ahneen** (ah-NEEN): greeting

**anama'eminensag** (ah-nam-ah'ay-min-ayns-ug): praying berries or ropes

**Anishinabe** (AH-nish-in-AH-bay): the original name for the Ojibwe or Chippewa people, a Native American group who originated in and live mainly in the northern North American woodlands. There are currently Ojibwe reservations in Michigan, Wisconsin, Minnesota, North Dakota, Ontario, Manitoba, Montana, and Saskatchewan

**Anishinabeg** (AH-nish-in-AH-bayg): the plural form of **Anishinabe**

**baka'akwen** (bah-kah-ah-kweh-n): chicken

**bezhig** (bay-zhig): one

**Biboonang** (Bib-oon-ung): Winter Spirit

**bine** (bin-ay): partridge

**binewag** (bin-ay-wug): the plural form of **bine**

**biwabik** (bii-wahb-ick): metal

**bizindaan** (bih-zin-dahn): listen

**Bwaan-akiing** (Bwahn-ah-keeng): the land of the Dakota and Lakota people, two other Native tribes

**Deydey** (DAY-day): Daddy

**dibi'** (dih-bih): I don't know where

**eya'** (ay-yah): yes

**gaawiin** (gah-WEEN): no

**geget** (GEH-geht): surely, or for emphasis, truly or really

**gidebwe** (ghih-day-bway): you speak the truth

**gigawaabamin** (gih-gah-WAH-bah-min): I will see you

**giigawedaa** (gee-gah-way-day): let's go home

**giiwedin** (gee-way-din): north

**gijigijigaaneshiinh** (gih-jih-gih-jih-gah-nay-shee): chickadee

**ginebigoog** (ghin-ay-big-oog): snakes

**Gizhe Manidoo** (Gih-zhay Man-ih-do): the great, kind spirit

154

**gookoosh** (goo-koosh): pig

**howaa** (HOW-ah): a sound of approval

**Iskigamizige-giizis** (Iss-kay-gah-mih-zih-gey-giizis): April

**majaan** (mah-jahn): go away!

**makak** (mah-KUK): a container of birchbark folded and often stitched together with basswood fiber. Ojibwe people use these containers today, especially for traditional feasts

**makakoon** (mah-kah-koon): the plural form of **makak**

**manoomin** (mah-NOH-min): wild rice; the word means "the good seed"

**mashi** (mahsh-ih): yet

**mashkiig** (maash-keeg): swampy place

**mekadewikonyewinini** (meh-kah-day-wih-kone-iy-eh-in-in-ih): black robe/priest

**memegwesiwag** (may-may-gway-see-wug): the plural form of **memegwesi**, little people

**miigwech** (mee-gwetch): thank you

**minopogwad** (min-oh-poh-gwud): it tastes good

**naanan** (nahn-an): five

**nashke** (nahsh-kay): look

**niiwin** (nee-win): four

**niizh** (neezh): two

**nimama** (nee-mama): my mama

**niswi** (niss-way): three

**Nokomis** (no-KOH-mis): grandmother
**Nookoo** (Noo-koo): shortened version of **Nokomis**
**waabooz** (WAH-booz): rabbit
**we'eh** (way-ay): namesake
**wigwam** (WIHG-wahm): a birchbark house
**wigwassi-wigamig** (wig-wass-ih-wig-ahm-ig): house
**Zhawanong** (Zhah-wah-nung): the South

# IT ALL BEGAN WITH OMAKAYAS.

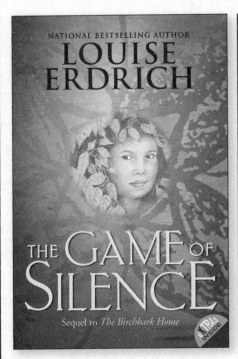

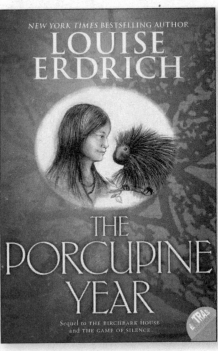

Before she was a mother, Omakayas was a girl
in search of a new home in books two and three
of the acclaimed Birchbark House series.

# SMALL THINGS HAVE GREAT POWER.

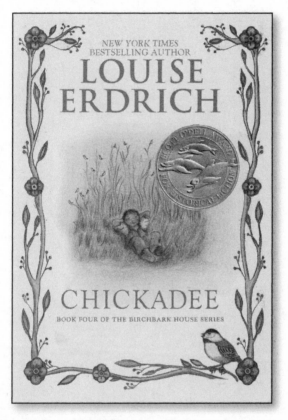

In book four of this award-winning series,
the unthinkable has happened—twins Makoons
and Chickadee have been separated.

**HARPER**
*An Imprint of HarperCollinsPublishers*

www.harpercollinschildrens.com